ESCAPING WITH WEST

A CLOSED DOOR MILITARY ROMANTIC SUSPENSE

EXCEPTIONAL MISSION UNIT : THE CARDINALS

CLAIRE CAIN

Cover design by Jess Mastorakos - Jess@jessmastorakos.com

EBOOK ISBN: 978-1-954005-51-8

PRINT ISBN: 978-1-954005-52-5

For my spy-lovin' gals. Here's to us! And cheers to you ladies who are actually out there living this life, doing the work of these types of organizations or married to the people who do. Can you tell us—Is Ethan Hunt really that fast?

CHAPTER ONE

Emily

Three hours.

I could smile and glad-hand for another three hours and then move on with my life, with this place. One last fancy gala, and my official duties would be done for the weekend. And after that? Only another few weeks before I left the US Embassy in Budapest behind and took... whatever job I decided to take next. Things were still up in the air in terms of specifics. Stateside? Definitely. More specific than that? No clue. Not how I preferred it, but that's how things stood.

"Everything on time with the catering?" Lucinda, the ambassador's admin, blinked at me over her iPad of wonders.

I swear, the woman could probably activate the nuclear package with that thing. "Yes, all good to go."

"I hope so." She peered at me hard over the infernal

device. "Because we really can't have this go wrong. Take my word for it, there are eyes on tonight, and you know we can't have any more bad press here."

Bad press as in a missing woman and the failure to acknowledge it until someone went to stateside media? *Yeah.* Someone tipped off the news outlets, and they'd been peppering the embassy officials for interviews, which put necessary but far-too-late pressure on them to respond. *Pretty bad*, I'd say, even after all the scrambling to find her, which had yet to happen.

"Of course. I'll go double-check everything again."

I smiled in the too-thin way I employed when I really wanted to roll my eyes and put someone in their place. I was good at my job, contrary to what little overzealous prisses like Lucinda thought. Being the newest here and leaving after a year might make me less of a badass in her eyes, but it didn't mean I was incompetent, particularly since this was only ever a year-long posting for me.

She simply nodded, evidently placated, and bustled away in her burgundy evening gown, off to terrorize the next unsuspecting government employee made to do her bidding for tonight's event. Good riddance and good luck to them.

A sigh escaped as my eyes wandered after her, taking in the gathering crowd. It'd be a full house tonight, and the ambassador liked to get everyone in place before he and his wife arrived with the guest of honor—tonight, an American pop star who happened to be world-famous and playing the Papp László Sportaréna tomorrow.

Everyone was dressed in their evening wear—tuxes and glittering gowns around every corner. The people became a blur, all blending together in their sparkle and contrast, like a fancy ball scene turned to one-point-five speed. They were all blissfully ignorant of the tension brewing within the embassy staff—the pressure to have this event go perfectly and make a show that there were no security issues here.

Nope. Nothing to see here, folks! Never mind if the unspoken consensus on why Janie Simmons hadn't returned to work was because she'd likely been human-trafficked. And the only reason anyone was actually acknowledging it was precisely because of the external pressures. The ambassador wasn't all bad, but everyone from the top down seemed unwilling to be upfront about the reality that Janie was missing and she hadn't simply taken a long vacation without telling anyone.

No one wanted to admit she'd likely been *taken*, and the ambassador had been working on reassuring the staff and Janie's parents that everything was fine. What it all added up to was a whole lot of hemming and hawing, which felt like stalling for time while, presumably, someone searched for her. And apparently, while we held this ball showing everything was totally fine.

Riiiight.

Where was Liam Neeson and his *very particular set of skills* when we needed him? Plus, Janie's disappearance threw into question at least one other staffer's sudden exit.

My time here had been hard, and not in a fun, challenging way. As a woman who's fairly comfortable with solitude and living alone, the move to Budapest had been surprisingly empty of the adventure I usually felt when assuming a new position. I'd left the world of education and now was simply a GS—General Schedule aka government employee. It'd been a small step up on the ladder, yay, but the work itself had been nondescript drudgery save planning an event that would take place after I left in a few weeks.

Maybe because my time in Germany had been so full of friendship and witnessing the growth of my friends and their relationships, I'd become restless with my wanderer's approach to life.

Happily, I'd be peacing out and on to a new posting with the potential for far longer than one year in T-minus six weeks. This place had been both hard on me, and lately, genuinely concerning and difficult to handle in terms of the risk it felt like we all faced. I'd miss a lot about Budapest—I'm looking at you, goulash—but not this frisson that'd taken hold over the last few months and only intensified the last two weeks since Janie had left.

See? Even my brain had tried to absorb the narrative that she'd left without telling anyone, without resigning, without making arrangements for her stuff, instead of being straight-up kidnapped. The alternative... Well, best not to think of it. I did not envy the team responsible for dealing with this issue.

After slipping into the restrooms, I straightened an arrangement of flowers and tucked a tightly rolled hand towel back into the basket holding them. The embassy was all kinds of fancy tonight. It was normally a beautiful build-ing, but the floral arrangements and bustling catering staff were enough to make it all feel like a grand exclamation point on my almost-year time here. Like this is what living abroad working for an embassy is supposed to be like. The grandeur, the glamour, the glittery swirl of it all. I'd had a few of these moments, but not as many as I'd hoped. And, again, they felt a bit empty lately.

Or maybe, *I* did.

But tonight, I was determined to feel good. Nothing was

going to stop me from enjoying the glitz this evening because I'd pep-talked my way into that mindset every minute I spent getting ready.

Maybe it was also because I looked hot. I wouldn't normally be so bold, but seriously. I looked *good* tonight. Would the evening be spent flirting with an equally hot date whilst resisting the urge to cringe anytime Lucinda approached and tried to question whether I'd done the duties she'd assigned despite my not technically being at all related to her chain of command? *No.*

A girl could dream. Sadly, tonight, I was on my own—and yes, I could see the trend of my dissatisfaction and lack of companionship. My local friend József would've been a great date, but he had plans already when I mentioned it a while back, and all of my other friends were going to be here by virtue of their working at the embassy, too. So, solo as usual.

But you know what? This shouldn't have been an issue. I'd been on my own. Minus a failed attempt or two at dating, I hadn't had a serious relationship since I'd lived at Fort Campbell. That'd been nearly six years ago, and just thinking of it made me feel tired.

It had all been by choice, though. I hadn't ever felt like I was missing out. I'd wanted flexibility, and once I made the move overseas, I wanted to stay. Working with a military population meant marrying a soldier was essentially catching, yet I had no interest. If I'd maintained my singledom after living on the tiny German base of Kugelfels and watching not one but *two* of my closest friends fall hard for soldiers, I felt reasonably secure it wouldn't happen now. The bug hadn't infected me there—I had developed immunity.

Had there been handsome soldiers who'd tempted me?

Sure. I was a red-blooded woman, and a man in uniform, even if they didn't look as good as the Marine uniform, did it for me. The Marines here at the embassy were all good guys, but we didn't run in the same circles since most of them were a decade younger than me or married.

I had to admit, this was one more reason I looked forward to a change. Being stateside would let me breathe, and it also meant I could meet a nice banker or teacher or *whatever* not-a-soldier and settle down and stay. Military wife life was not for me. Suburban mom? Why not?

It'd be great. Perfect, really. Steady and predictable with not having to stress about deployments and moves I didn't feel like making for my own career. I'd had enough of the drama of moving, of contemplating new skies and new horizons. Maybe I was getting too old for the wanderlust? I just knew I wanted to settle somewhere for a time, and yes, have a boring life for the foreseeable future.

And I'd figure out *where* in the states I wanted to land any day now. Any minute. I needed to make final arrangements, and I needed to accept one of the two positions I'd been offered and had been delaying confirming. But for now? Fancy party time.

I studied my reflection, tracing a finger over the dark eyebrow perfectly arched over my onyx lashes and shimmery shadow. *Makeup on point.* I slid a manicured nail along the hair at the side of my head. Raising my brows, I stuck out my tongue at the woman preening back at me, then waved her away. Rude jerk did the same right back to me.

With an eye roll at my ridiculous inner monologue, I pushed out the door and checked my watch. Thirteen minutes until the ambassador and his wife would arrive. Five more minutes for most of the riffraff to show up before they tightened security all the way down ahead of the bigwigs' arrivals.

Something was in the air tonight. A shimmering sense of possibility hung in every room I walked into, almost like all of us were waiting for someone to yell "Surprise!" when we entered. I'd take it over the dread and worry that'd permeated the place lately, for sure, but it set me on an odd edge as I milled around.

Maybe everyone innately knew this event had popped up on the calendar last minute to provide a classy, *we're all fine here!* optic. Maybe they could tell coaxing mega pop star Bri Williamson to meet and greet here was silly and just an excuse to seem like nothing was amiss.

People were chatting loudly, as though they'd already helped themselves to the open bar for more than one round. Couldn't be the case, since no alcohol would be served until the guest of honor arrived, and yet the place was positively abuzz. Bri Williamson, American heartthrob and dreamy pop star extraordinaire, had to be the reason.

He seemed nice and I looked forward to meeting him, but I had this gut feeling that tonight had something in store. I couldn't explain the niggling any better. Most likely, it was the anticipation of moving and being on the precipice of settling somewhere I hoped I wouldn't feel compelled to leave after a year.

Or maybe, as a member of the staff, the low-level anxiety that one of us would be next and we had no real concept of what it even meant had slipped into my awareness more than I'd realized.

"No, no, pardon me," a woman said, a little too loudly somewhere behind me.

I glanced over my shoulder, taking in the woman patting a tall man's tuxedoed shoulder, and froze.

Him.

The man in a perfect black tux nodded and turned to greet the woman's plus-one, regrettably forcing his face away from me.

But I'd seen his profile, the heavy brow, sharp jaw, and kind face. I knew that face.

Holy Hungarian goulash, it was actually *him.*

I'd thought about *him* for months. *Years at this point,* I admitted inwardly.

I'd met him during my time working at the education center on Kugelfels Army base in Germany. He'd come in dressed in civilian clothes to take a handful of language tests no one in their right mind would take all in one week.

And he'd pointed his glorious intellect at me and pulled the trigger by passing them all with nearly native-level fluency.

Can we stop and take a moment to appreciate a man who is really, *really* good at something? With the rampant mediocrity of so many men these days, meeting one who made my brain short-circuit with his smarts proved more than a little bit of a turn on.

Like, a lotta bit.

But that's not where we stop, folks. Because the guy was absolutely *my type.* I'm talking dark hair a little longish on the top, beard—longer then than it was now, if my glimpse was accurate—and stunning blue eyes.

Le sigh. How I did love pretty blue eyes on a handsome man.

Oh and also, let's be clear. The guy was perfectly mannered, endlessly courteous, and he smelled *great.* Why would I know such a thing? As is wont to happen in a military education center building, the *on-their-last-legs* computers used for testing had a malfunction during one of his tests and I had to reset it. He stayed in his seat but slid back and I leaned over—yes, it was awkward—and typed in the proctor code to deal with the issue. Long story short? He smelled like fresh laundry and minty chewing gum.

None of this *he smelled like a man* business. No. Give me laundry detergent and mint gum any day of the freaking week. That's a man I want to snuggle up with. You can keep your mysterious man scent with a hint of sandalwood, because honestly, what does sandalwood even smell like?

I'd ranted to my dear friend Bec Jones about the unfairness of it all. God had served up a perfectly delicious man and had I slipped him my number? Asked him if he had dinner plans while he was in town?

No. I'd done what I always did—the completely professional thing. I was great at my work, and I'd been great every day he'd tested that memorable week—no tongue-tied awkwardness in the face of Beauty and the Brains.

He'd left with "Thank you, I really appreciate all your help, Ms. Wender," and I'd said, "Good luck, Mr. West." And that was it.

He'd left Kugelfels amidst rumors he worked for EMU —the Exceptional Mission Unit. And I'd tried to keep from fantasizing about what would've happened if I'd prioritized my own happiness ahead of professional duty.

I hadn't heard a whisper about Ryan West since, hadn't seen him. And trust, I'd kept an ear and eye out.

Not even a nibble of news anywhere to be found for nearly two years.

Until tonight.

CHAPTER TWO

West

Ambassador Kline shook my hand. "Glad to meet you. Did you meet my friend Bri Williamson?"

I tipped my head to the man in question. "Pleasure. My sister's a huge fan."

Williamson smiled and nodded. "Tell her thank you. I have the best fans in the world."

Amazingly, it didn't sound canned, nor overly familiar. Bri and I went back a ways—we'd worked closely on a mission a few months ago, and he'd been solid. More than. As a pop star, I never would've expected him to agree to help our joint mission with the Kappa Sector, a secret department within the CIA, to infiltrate notorious arms dealer Maksim Volkov's Russian compound. But the man rose to the occasion, our team succeeded in planting small date-sweeping bots in his servers, and we'd been rolling in information ever since.

Granted, what we'd gleaned hadn't broken anything open, and now it appeared the US government had a leak playing right into Volkov's hands. Bri couldn't help us with any of this here, but it was certainly nice of him to show up and be the excuse for this little sham of a party, and thank goodness he could act better than most musicians. If the attendees only knew they were here to make it look like everything was fine and that far more than a missing woman was under investigation right under their noses, they'd likely be a little less carefree.

I did my best to check off this meet and get on with it. The clock was ticking, and I'd need to meet my team in the south side bathrooms in no more than seven minutes. We had a window of opportunity to exploit just after this introduction, while most people were still in the receiving line and we wouldn't be missed. If we botched the timing, we'd be hard-pressed to accomplish this first mission, and though we always had one, I didn't particularly want to resort to Plan B.

Plan B was breaching the building much later tonight. We'd be dealing with security from the outside instead of the inside, and while it wouldn't necessarily be *harder*, it was much nicer to walk in the front doors.

The ambassador himself wasn't particularly under suspicion, even though we knew someone here was leaking information and maybe had a hand in the recent disappearances. It was less likely to be someone high-profile like him and far more to be some lower-level State Department grunt who needed cash. I didn't see ideology playing a part here. MICE—Money, Ideology, Corruption, Ego—stood for the levers used to get someone to switch sides or defect. Corruption and ego? Not enough high-level players to recruit here. So money had to be it.

If I got lucky tonight, I might just find the intel we needed and suss out the rat.

"Ah, Emily. Did you get a chance to meet Bri Williamson?" The ambassador widened his arm to fold someone into our small group.

"Pleased to meet you. Thanks for coming tonight."

My eyes flicked to the woman next to me as Williamson responded.

Oh. Damn. I knew that voice. I knew this woman.

And she knew me. The real me.

What were the odds I'd make it out of here without this blowing all to hell in my face?

In an instant, my memory vaulted me back a year and a half to knocking on the door of the testing center at the Kugelfels military base education building. And there she was, Emily Wender. Dark brown hair to her shoulders and a bright smile.

Extending her hand, she'd apologized for the confusion and broke the news that contrary to what the person who'd scheduled me a few days prior had said, I couldn't take all of the tests I had planned in the same week. She'd explained the DoD had policies in place to limit overlap and prevent testing burnout, which increased success rates.

She'd seemed genuinely perturbed the testing center manager had allowed this and at the same time, truly regretful to tell me no, but determined to do so.

I should've been irritated, since I'd gotten express permission from the other person, but when she moved to sit at her desk, I'd taken a seat across from her. Watching her click through screens, reviewing her amended plan, she'd hardly given me a second look until I said, "I'll take them all. I'll pass them with a four or better. If I fail anything at any point, you can use that to justify canceling the rest of my tests."

It was then she hit me with her endless eyes, and I saw the flare of curiosity as she fully took me in. I didn't look like the average soldier she tested—I hadn't come in uniform since I rarely wore one. Slacks, button-up shirt, and a trimmed beard made me look more like a contractor or GS than a soldier. She'd eyed me for a minute, during which my pulse had jumped as I drank in her full lips and the slope of her neck and the soft scent perfuming the office, and then she'd agreed.

I was used to getting my way, but it had been the challenge in her eyes, the desire to see me succeed and prove her wrong, that had pulled at me. She hadn't flirted or blushed or leaned over to give me a glimpse of her chest—all things I'd experienced a hundred times. She'd kept going, professional and polite with a friendly conversational tone that set me at ease and told me she was, too. It'd made so little sense, but I'd just... liked her. So much. Right away.

Every second I'd spent in that building afterward was seared into my memory, including handing her my ID to check me in and having her mumble "Ryan West" as though she liked the sound of it. Honestly, it was a testament to my training and ability to focus that I did pass all the tests because simply knowing she was sitting on the other side of the plexiglass while I tapped away at the computer had been enough to make even the French exam a challenge in spots.

I could hear North's voice in my head, though only in my imagination since we were off the net for now. *Approximately point-two percent she doesn't detonate this in our faces, dummy.* Our resident numbers wiz would calculate the odds of just about anything, not to mention he was also our CMOE guy, clandestine methods of entry practically his love language, so he could get *into* just about anywhere.

"And have you met Mr. Jacobs?" Ambassador Kline, excellent host that he was, hammered in the nail.

"I don't believe I have," she said, shifting her attention to me.

And *yep*. She recognized me, too. And she definitely *had* met me, but she'd lied, straight out.

"Excellent. Ms. Emily Wender, one of our embassy's best and a great favorite among the locals, please meet Mr. Ryan Jacobs."

Her lashes fluttered. "Mr. Jacobs, is it?"

I didn't speak, only held her gaze. She knew very well he'd introduced me with a different name than the one I'd tested under at the base in Germany. And if she wanted to, she'd blow this whole thing open with a word since Ambassador Kline clearly knew her better than most.

"Jacobs's here with a training group from DoD—doing some basic safety training for us next week, right?"

I nodded, determined to keep things vague and, if possible, redirect interest to Williamson, who stood by congenially while the introductions were made.

"Well. Very nice to meet you, Mr. Jacobs."

Her dark eyes skated over my face and, I kid you not, twinkled back at me. *She's enjoying this.* Or at least, she wasn't about to bust my cover.

A thrill I'd only experienced when looking at her snaked through me, demanding I step closer to her, learn more about why she's here, anything. Or maybe pick up from where we left off in Kugelfels. Fortunately, my body didn't go along with that impulse.

I nodded again, determined not to say another word in

the presence of this woman or risk getting roped into a longer conversation. I didn't have the time—less than three minutes to meet the team. Plus, based on my even noticing her glittery gaze, I couldn't stand to be near her another minute, or I'd end up caught in the thrall of her eyes and lips and... everything. I'd never once had trouble focusing while on mission, and I wasn't about to tempt fate and myself by staying here with the one woman I couldn't forget inches from me.

The fact that I'd managed to pass my language tests with her right outside the testing room tapping away on her computer and being solicitous and kind qualified as a miracle. When my computer had frozen and she'd reset it the first day, she'd leaned over next to me and a warm, subtle lavender linen scent had damn near incapacitated me, it'd caused such instant hunger in me. When she'd made charming small talk while the computer restarted, I'd felt it. This thing I'd never felt with anyone and something I didn't think I'd be able to live without—longing, home, desire, comfort, interest, delight...

Walking away from that pull between us had been a second miracle, no doubt. But I'd finished my week of testing there in Germany rather than going back to the compound in North Carolina like I normally would've so I was ready to pivot and join my team back in the Middle East as quickly as possible.

Sometimes, I wondered what would've happened if I'd had more time... if I'd asked her to grab a drink after that last test on Friday instead of rolling out of Germany on a flight hours later. I would've asked and she probably would've turned me down at first since she struck me as strictly professional, and that would likely seem rather unprofessional. But maybe I would've found a way to convince her, or maybe she would've decided just one drink wasn't a problem...

And tonight? We'd call it Round Three. I did not have time to get hung up on Emily Wender, nor could I afford to explain to her why she'd just been introduced to me under a different name.

Cue evasive action. Handy that I'd had a fair amount of practice with such things.

North gave me a subtle nod from across the room and I took my chance. "If you'll excuse me, I need to go rescue my partner. It was an honor to meet you, Ambassador. Same to you, Williamson." I tipped my chin down at Emily. "Ma'am."

"Of course. Nice to meet you," the ambassador said, leaning to listen as his wife whispered in his ear.

Williamson raised his glass to me, eyebrow quirking slightly like he was enjoying the show.

"Lovely to meet you, Mr. Jacobs," Emily said, catching my eye and sending a streak of heat throughout me before I turned.

I crushed my response to her—the words I wanted to say, the physical reaction to her nearness, and that sass making me want to pin her against a wall and kiss her 'til she had no more words.

Down, boy.

The adrenaline spike courtesy of the close call with her had me slightly off-kilter, but the walk away provided a breath to get my mind right. *Ninety seconds now.*

I made it to North in a few strides, taking my time to move at a measured pace.

"Someone looks piqued."

I glared at him, but he just smiled and blinked back at me through his thick frames.

"Seriously, what's up?"

"I'm made, but she's not talking. We need to move the timeline up."

North glanced back to where I'd been. "How does she—"

"Later. Point is, that ticking clock just lost time. Let's move."

He nodded, and in an instant, his eyes drooped, shoulders slumping enough to make him look unsteady. He let his wrist slacken just enough so his glass of whiskey dribbled out a drop on the floor.

"One too many already? Can't take you anywhere." I made an embarrassed face and nodded to the couple standing a few feet away. "My apologies."

They shook their heads like it was nothing, then inched away from us. No need, since I guided North away by the elbow, down the hall as though I'd take him to the men's restroom. We'd prepped the route, and as soon as we were out of the receiving room and around the corner, he straightened as we met South just inside the men's restroom.

"You're early. Good thing I'm a Boy Scout, yeah?"

His thick Boston accent made it all sound so casual. He handed us the clear earbuds we'd use for communication. The intel as to how they'd stepped up security and had more complex scans to enter the building had been wrong—they'd put in the order but hadn't implemented yet, but we'd taken every precaution anyway. South had come in the "back way," which was just about his favorite thing on Earth along with doing basic surgical procedures in odd locations and maybe eating, so he wasn't complaining.

Tucking the comm into my ear, I spoke. "We're in. Copy?"

East responded immediately. "Copy."

Our man of few words was, inevitably, our communications expert. It worked perfectly since no one wanted a chatterbox crowding the network.

"I'm heading up. You're out, South. And North?"

He lurched and dumped whiskey down his shirt. "Whoopsie. Guess I better scrub that out."

With one last nod, I peeked out the door, then exited and slipped around the corner to the elevator. If anyone came looking for us, they'd find North taking his sweet, fakely inebriated time scrubbing out his shirt. South would leave the way he came, but not until I made it back down the elevator with what we needed.

Based on the woman missing and some of the weapons movements we'd been tracking through the region, we'd sifted through intel we'd gotten from Volkov's servers and had a strong suspicion we could find evidence of a mole responsible for selling government secrets amongst the US embassy staff. We'd been reconning all week, but the first move was to get a look before anyone realized we were watching—in other words, while they were all downstairs partying with a pop star and just finding out we'd arrived for our cover story instruction on safety.

The elevator dinged and clanked open. Pressing the top button, I watched the doors slide closed inch by inch until they froze and bounced back open.

A colorful array of expletives shot through my mind courtesy of our resident foulmouthed Bostonian. Or, formerly foulmouthed, and now... food-mouthed? He'd shifted from actual swearing to things like *Son of a home-style biscuit* and *What the flourless chocolate torte are you thinking?*

In my own mind, my words sounded like his new

method, too, and though I didn't make a peep, I had to work to smooth out my features as a woman with a short silvery-blond bob and iPad slipped into the box with a serene smile followed by—why was I even surprised, at this point?—Emily Wender.

My stomach clenched. This was really about to go down in flames, wasn't it?

The woman with the iPad looked up in a double take before her stern brow wrinkled. "Pardon us, but are you in the right—"

"Did you want me to submit the report from last month tomorrow?" Emily asked her, resolutely ignoring me.

"I—what? Didn't you do that last week?" She gave Emily a look like she was an absolute idiot.

Dislike hit me instantly. Unusual, considering I typically took a while to evaluate people, but this woman pulled into sharp focus immediately. The curl of her upper lip as she waited for Emily's response honestly made me want to stare her down, but engaging in any way would only bring her attention back to me.

"You know what? You're so right. I've been so distracted by tonight and the symposium in a few months, it must've slipped my mind."

The woman gave Emily another disgusted look. "You really need to get a handle on yourself, child. You're not going to get anywhere with that kind of forgetfulness." She gazed back down to her screen.

Emily's eyes narrowed at her, then found me.

Yep, still gorgeous. Her dark lashes and the expert sweep of makeup over her lids made her look particularly alluring. Her lips were the color of the inside of a red plum, and though the only contact we'd ever had was a handshake the first time we met and when I left the last day back in Germany, I could practically taste her.

Well, crap.

"You are so right, Lucinda. I'll do better."

I'd already made a mental note to check into this Lucinda woman—I'd have East check her when he ran Emily's background and history, which he'd have to do since there was no way this wasn't cycling back on me. We were here for a few weeks, and now, I was in Emily's debt. I'd liked her from the beginning, but I didn't assume anything. As for Lucinda, she was likely too high up the chain to be the culprit, but never say never.

The elevator dinged loudly as it arrived at their floor and the doors pulled open. Lucinda beelined out, eyes glued to the device. Emily lingered, like she might steal a moment to say something. I couldn't risk her critical companion overhearing, particularly since she seemed to have forgotten about me.

The doors began to close, and I stuck out a hand to force them back and hold them at bay. She gave me her eyes, all dark and a kind of hypnosis I wished I had time for. Why was there never time with her? Was that what made me feel this way—somehow knowing nothing could ever happen between us whenever I ran into her?

Her gaze swept over my face, then returned to meet mine. My chest tightened, like the pressure increased, like that flat-line silence just before an explosion you only recognize in retrospect. Her lips parted to speak, but the moment came to an arresting end another way.

"Emily, what on earth are you doing?" Lucinda had swung back around to see us. From her perspective, it wouldn't have looked like a loaded silence. It wouldn't look like a moment just before a leap.

Emily blinked and pressed her lips together before marching forward. "Maybe I'm getting sick or something."

The doors lurched closed as Lucinda said, "Maybe it was the handsome man you were practically drooling over? Take my word for it, he doesn't belong here. No idea what he's doing but—"

"That must be it—"

And it's all I got of them. The cables pulled the car up, up, and a few seconds later, the doors clanked open yet again. She'd saved my hide twice in half an hour, and I wouldn't soon forget it.

But now, it was time to do a little research.

In my ear, East prompted me right as I stepped onto the top floor. "Time to go to work, West."

"Roger. Let's do it."

CHAPTER THREE

Emily

I woke up the next morning with the pleasant feeling of relief when remembering the last big embassy event of my tenure here in Budapest could be marked completed. I had the symposium still, but that would actually happen after I moved stateside, so it didn't feel the same. And so, relief.

Okay, fine. Maybe not only relief.

A little regret. Or if not regret, then a small sense of missing out on something.

Why?

Because of Ryan Jacobs, aka Ryan West, hottest language nerd of them all. I'd never expected to see him in real life again—I'd given up on him returning to Kugelfels when I hit the year mark and he hadn't been back. He knew my name after interacting for a week as his testing administrator. If he'd been at all interested, he could've called the ed center, knowing I worked there. E-mailed. Maybe sent a carrier pigeon since that seemed like something he might actually know how to do.

And yes, I knew his name, too, but it would be a misuse of personal info. Not professional, not my jam, even if the man was absolutely and completely the very definition of my jam. The confidence, the voice, the size of his hands, the closely-trimmed beard, and knowing what a fantastic head full of languages he had...

Ja-yum, two syllables, emphasis on the *yum*.

But then there he was. Shaking hands with the ambassador and Bri freaking Williamson. And there I was, taking in the fact that Ambassador Kline had introduced him as Ryan Jacobs and barely being able to acknowledge one of the most popular current musical artists and *World's Sexiest Pop Star* like eleven hundred times over because *there. He. Was.*

Still gorgeous. Eyes the same bright blue looking right at me, full of interest and delight and a kind of intelligence that spoke to me on a cellular level. But he didn't say a word to me—not one!—until that "ma'am." He gave me a dapper nod like that would satisfy my endless curiosity. And then it clicked, of course, because I was above average intelligence and could put two and two together most of the time.

He'd been rumored to be Exceptional Mission Unit. Here he was being introduced under what I didn't think I was exaggerating in calling an alias. *Holy crap, he's on a mission!* Maybe he was CIA? But no, we were cooperating with them, and he wasn't State Department or he really wouldn't have been testing at Kugelfels those years ago. Though even as EMU, that wouldn't have made much sense. He'd looked much more... sturdy than a linguist analyst would be, at least based on those I'd met. But his acumen had been stunning, and his excellent manners, and the broad shoulders accompanying those things...

Clearly, I'd been enamored. And last night? He'd been up to something. He'd been working, and just the thought gave me a thrill as I dressed for the day. I loved a good spy story, and the idea that I now knew a man who was one in some form or another? It was just too dang cool! He totally had the handsome spy thing, or in the case of a soldier, operative thing, going on. But why had he been there? And was it EMU he was working for?

Whatever the case, he'd been there last night and he'd used a fake name. Ambassador Kline had said he'd be doing a training for *us*, which usually meant the embassy staff, and he was with DoD. So he was undercover as a Department of Defense trainer of some sort?

Color me intrigued.

Then he was gone. I'd searched the room, catching sight of his back as he led away another man who looked far too good in his tux to be anyone but a fellow EMU guy. So I'd hustled—and I do mean the word because the man was tall and his strides covered about three of mine in the heels I'd worn—after him.

Who'd foiled me? Lucinda, inevitably. But somewhere in my brain, above the stringed instruments playing Franz List and the din of conversation, the elevator dinged, and in my gut I *knew* he was the one who'd called it.

Lucinda had met my steps with her own, staying right with me and claiming she needed to run to her desk after I'd mentioned popping upstairs to grab something. I couldn't shake her and barely caught the car, but as the doors creaked back, they'd revealed Ryan West, legit international man of mystery.

Just thinking about him standing there with his glittery

eyes in that tux sent my stomach to the floor. Even the mundane chatter of fellow pedestrians on the sidewalk of my street couldn't stave off a slight flush at remembering his casual stance, that assured way of standing like he belonged there and shouldn't be suspected of being there even though he had no fathomable reason to be anywhere but at the party, if that.

By the time I made it through the busiest section of my walking commute, I was ready to collapse. I hadn't slept like I'd planned—an utter waste of an alarm clock-free morning after an event when we had a late call to work. Between seeing Ryan Jacobs slash West and worrying over all the issues the leadership in the embassy might be covering up with a party like that, or with bringing in someone like him, my brain had been buzzing nonstop.

I *hadn't* thought about all the things I needed to do to get settled and start life back in the US in a matter of weeks. When I'd turned to myself, I'd spent a disappointing amount of time waffling about my future. As someone who generally had a vision and focus in life, I'd lost the drive during my time here. I hated owning up to that, because it made me feel weak and like I couldn't handle the challenge, but in some ways, that was the truth. I might not like it, but why else had I failed to find my stride here?

Not that anyone I worked with would say such a thing. The ambassador himself had been encouraging to me, and I was nowhere near his office in the building itself. My direct report boss and everyone else I worked with had seemed stunned when I'd submitted notice I was leaving instead of extending for another year.

But to me, it'd felt right. I'd come to terms with the fact that the adventure I'd sought here had fallen flat and it wasn't Budapest's fault. It was mine. I was ready for something different, and I couldn't find it bouncing around from place to place.

I was smart enough to know my lack of desire for roots likely stemmed from my childhood. There was nothing traumatic or particularly sad, though. My parents had loved me in the way they knew how—by working to provide. For them, it'd meant constantly working to make ends meet, around the clock, which left me to myself most of the time.

And so, I'd been alone, and not by choice. As I grew, I wore my independence like armor and left home as soon as I could, forging my way independently to alleviate myself from my parents' list of burdens, and also to prove I would choose relying on myself, being with myself, even if no one else did.

Some of that had softened as I'd found my place in the world—a working professional with a steady income and no one else to worry about. I'd picked up friends who slipped underneath my distancing techniques—Bec, Livie, Katie, Summer—but I'd always been fine just being with me. Until some of those friends who all had events in their pasts that made them wary of connection had found ways to open up to love and looking forward, and a small voice inside me started asking, "Why not me?"

Partly it was because I hadn't met anyone I even considered wanting to try with, so I felt safe. And then Ryan West walked into the ed center and blew that out of the water.

So last night, I should've been basking in the relief of finishing up this event and finally nailing down which job I'd take, and therefore where I was moving, in the US. Instead, I'd relived every second of interacting with a man I'd likely never see again, an event that had exactly zero bearing on the rest of my life.

Actually...

I might see him again. I could even possibly see him in the building today, if he really was there to teach a class. And if not...

EMU is part of Army special operations.

Fort Liberty is home of special operations.

So... Ryan West might actually be stationed at one of the places where I planned to move.

Okay, yikes. We do not make decisions based on men who disappear into the night with their giant brains and who have clearly demonstrated their lack of interest in us. No, we do not.

"You have got to get a grip, woman," I said aloud to myself, because that's what normal women did in the middle of the street on the way to meet a friend. *Ryan West is not for you.*

Just thinking the man's name had me off-kilter, so the thought I might encounter him somewhere around where I'd be living?

Granted, this line of thought had done nothing for me in the long year after I'd first met him. He'd never shown back up in Germany. Why would I assume, on one of the largest military bases in the US where I had yet to step foot, he'd materialize and be interested in even having a conversation?

But maybe he'll be around here for that class...

"Focus on the now, Wender."

Yes, spoke aloud on the street again, forcing my eyes open wider and willing myself to perk up. As a woman who'd moved a lot, changed jobs fairly often, and frequently felt like I was rebuilding my life from scratch, I'd mastered the art of being present now—well, mostly. Part of the key to making transitions smooth was diving into life, the here and now of it, and digging in deep. I considered this one of my fortes, though I wondered if perhaps that mentality had kept me from letting my roots dig in deep enough to find *more*.

In theory, part of this skill set meant *not* checking out a full six weeks before departure. But the way I'd been mentally absent from my job here, failing to really connect with any friends other than one girlfriend at the embassy and one local more recently... it confirmed it was time to get back to the US, at least for a while.

For now, I should focus on wrapping things up here in Budapest. It really was a lovely city, and I had a few more weeks of normalcy before things went wild with an international move and readjusting to American culture again. I loved routines and predictable patterns, and the best thing for me was to jump into the day with both feet.

And the second-best thing would be to forget Ryan West Jacobs Whatever even existed.

Up ahead, József raised his hand in greeting from a small table in front of one of the multitude of adorable restaurants hidden on every street.

"Hello, Emily." He rose from his seat, towering over me at several inches above six feet. He had thick brows and an angular face with nicely styled blond hair and dark eyes—certainly handsome in an approachable, accessible way.

"Hello, friend. It's great to see you. Thank you for getting a table." He was always early—I had never once beaten him to a place, and I tended to be right on time.

"My pleasure," he said, his accent heavy and dragging at the *l* in the word.

I'd miss the sounds of Hungarian and accented English when I left.

A waitress approached and spoke in rapid Hungarian. I'd picked up a few phrases and had my usual order prepared, but once József had spoken, she smiled at me. "What for you, miss?"

Inwardly, I chuckled. I'd never escape the humbling reality that I did not blend in. Somehow, I broadcasted my American-ness, despite doing everything I could to be as nondescript and unremarkable as possible. It was both a safety concern and a point of pride, but it'd worked far better in Germany than it did here, for some reason.

I ordered my tea and pastry and turned to my friend, glad for a moment to think about something other than work and hot Army men, when a voice interrupted us.

"Is that you, Emily?"

My stomach flipped, and I turned to see a man sauntering up with a wide smile and a look on his face like he hadn't seen me in years instead of hours.

So much for not thinking about Ryan West.

CHAPTER FOUR

West

I'd happened upon Emily right as she approached a man sitting at a table. Looked like they had a friendly rapport, but no hug or kiss at greeting, and I wouldn't acknowledge the satisfaction that snuck through me. I couldn't pretend I wasn't glad to see her for the second time in twenty-four hours, even if this *glad* feeling felt a bit more like *excited* and *nervous* and *curious* and *greedy for more*.

"Do not engage."

North's voice came through the comm speaker tucked in my ear loud and clear.

"Don't do it, Westy. You can't do what you need to do with this guy there."

South's logic was sound. I hadn't *accidentally* found Emily. I'd been waiting on the most logical path based on East's background check of her and some light digging he did, and sure enough, we'd narrowed down that she likely took this route to get from her apartment to the embassy. Most people were creatures of habit, and Emily was no different. We needed to have a quick chat before we interacted again because, cliché though it may have been, she knew too much.

In other words, I needed to talk with her and level with her. First, I wanted her to acknowledge she had noticed the disparity in my name. It sounded obvious, but if she refused to let on that she knew my name was in fact Ryan West and not, as Ambassador Kline introduced me, Ryan Jacobs, that might hint if she was going to try to leverage this information.

Based on her response to this issue, we'd go from there, either sliding some pressure onto her to see if she had anything to do with the leaks, though I didn't suspect that, or alternately, confirming she had no plans to share my true identity and eliciting a promise not to disclose that information at any point.

I grunted, squinting at the scene of Emily smiling at this man, wondering what he wanted from her. And make no mistake, he definitely wanted *her* based on the way his eyes lit up, but my gut told me he wanted something else, too.

"Let's check on this guy, too."

South snorted, and North groaned dramatically, but East spoke low and steady. "József Molnár. Twenty-five. Hungarian national. Has lived in Budapest a little over a year. Appears to have known Emily for about two months, give or take, and he's bffs with an LES."

"Ah, should mean he's been vetted by State, so that's good," South said, chuckling.

If this guy was friends with a Locally Employed Staff of the embassy, that meant he'd been background checked by the State Department. I didn't need to worry as much, but I still kept watching as the guy pulled out Emily's chair, then took his seat.

"Do. Not. Approach." North said it with such authority, like he was in charge.

He wasn't. *I* was. Poor sweet North.

Again, sound logic in some sense. I shouldn't be interacting with her outside the embassy on the off chance someone who witnessed our meeting last night might realize we knew each other outside the terse exchange at the party. But the odds of that were slim, and what if charming József here was someone we should be getting to know? Something told me he was bad news, and I never ignored my gut. He might've been vetted by the State Department, but that didn't mean I shouldn't get a little closer. What better way to meet him?

"But he looks so nice. I think I will." I pushed off the wall and wandered toward the small table as the waitress scuttled away with their order.

"Is that you, Emily?" I said as I approached, ignoring the clamor from North's protests and South's disbelieving laugh in my ear.

Her mouth dropped open and she blinked, then smiled politely. "Ah, Ryan. Good to see you."

Approval hummed in me. She'd used my first name. No intention to figure out which name I'd be using today, just the reliable first name I'd used in both cases. Smart and strategic.

Also a good reason why we tended to use consistent first names for all our covers. No need to remember two names when one would do. Why be Ryan West in real life and George Jacobs as a cover when I could simply be Ryan Jacobs?

"This is a friend?" József asked in accented English as he and Emily both stood to greet me.

Before she spoke, I slipped a hand around her waist and dropped a kiss to her cheek. Her quick intake of breath told me I'd surprised her, but likely not as much as I'd surprised myself. *What are you doing, idiot?*

North was going to murder me.

"Yes. Yeah. We're friends from work," Emily said, a small stutter-step in her words.

I held her gaze, her lovely brown eyes confused and more than a little alight with curiosity. No makeup today after last night's glamourous look, and still, she was gorgeous. If last night made me think about taking her out with her as my singular focus, today made me think about waking up next to her and being the one to make her tea.

Get back on track.

She waited with interest piqued in the lift of her brows, and I remembered how I'd liked that about her from the first day, the first meeting. She was expressive and whip-smart with a dry, frank sense of humor I wanted to drink down like cold beer after mowing the lawn in summer.

"Yes, we are." Maybe I was laying it on thick here, but I wanted József to step back. He'd crowded into Emily's space and that was a bit much.

My right? No.

Too bad for him.

"It's nice to meet you. I'm József."

He held out his hand just shy of invading the space between us. A bit pushy, but maybe he felt threatened by me. If his intention was to date Emily, he had to be experiencing sore disappointment about now. She'd never mentioned me, no doubt, and my greeting like a close old friend might've spooked him, or again, made him feel threatened.

Maybe he should.

"Likewise." I took his hand with a firm grip, and we shook once, then released.

A beat passed where we simply stood, and then József chuckled and stepped back. "Well, I've just recalled I have an early meeting, but I'll talk to you soon, Emily, yes?"

She blinked and shook her head as though coming out of a daze. "What? You haven't eaten yet."

He took another large step away from where we stood. "Oh, it's nothing. See you soon."

The waitress returned and began unloading her tray as Emily watched her friend retreat. I waited, curious to see what she'd do. Would she slap me? Yell at me? Walk away without a word?

As I was coming to realize she would do, Emily surprised me. She sat down, tucked her napkin in her lap, picked up her tea, and glanced up at me.

"You might as well sit since you ran him off."

A smile cracked wide open on my face, and I sat. "Is that what I did?"

Her lashes fluttered. "Isn't it?"

I took in her face, as lovely now as it had been last night, and didn't bother stifling a grin. "I think he ran off all on his own."

Her unimpressed look made me laugh, but when she reluctantly chuckled, I knew I'd won.

"I am sorry about that. I only meant to say hello." *And have a little chat one-on-one, which works out perfectly.*

"Oh, well. I'll see him again soon, I'm sure. We seem to run into each other all over the place." She sipped her coffee.

I filed that piece of information away. For now, we needed to cover a few things before North had a meltdown.

"It's good to see you," I said before I could stop myself, and my inner-ear audience groaned. Internally, I did, too. I shouldn't have started there. I shouldn't be doing any of this without a little more circumspection, but seeing her again after so long made me want to be a little reckless.

Not normal for me. Something I'd need to reflect on later when she wasn't sitting right in front of me.

Her brows flicked up, but a smile tugged at the corners of her mouth.

"Likewise." She studied me for a moment, then cupped her mug and asked, "I assume you can't say anything about... anything?"

"Correct. That's why I wanted to talk."

She made a face like she'd found me out. "I thought maybe this wasn't a coincidence."

"Coincidences are rare."

With a roll of her eyes, she shook her head. "Okay. What else do you need to say or... not say?"

"We've established we know each other. I'll be in the office for training for the next few days, and you may see us around the building. Since we've told your best bud József we know each other, we might as well continue that, but let's keep it vague. If anyone asks, we'll say it's from one of your past duty stations and leave it there."

She swallowed and nodded. "Are you in danger?"

Damn if she wasn't completely adorable. "I'll be just fine. Thanks for your concern."

She shrugged a little, as though to brush away any hint of worry she might've shown with her question. "Good to know."

"Out of curiosity, how did you meet József?"

She set down her cup on the saucer and gave me an incredulous look. "This is your business, why? Also, he's like ten years younger than you."

"Into younger men?"

She laughed—big and bold, her smile a lightning bolt. "You're ridiculous."

A crackle of static sliced into my ear before North ranted away, irritation ringing hot in every syllable. "She's right! You *are* ridiculous, and this whole conversation is nonsense. Get out of there before you embarrass yourself, man."

As if I didn't already know he was mad thanks to the last five minutes of complaining in my ear.

I shrugged a shoulder. "I'm simply curious."

She looked at me for a moment, likely trying to figure out what I was after, and finally filled in the blank.

"He ran into me. We were walking and he was looking at a map and he knocked into me and dropped his stuff. He was so embarrassed and then asked me how to get to this café, actually, and I showed him since I was on the way. He was meeting someone who didn't show, and we were sitting a table apart and ended up chatting. He's new to the city and... well, anyway, there you have it."

Actual concern hit right as South swore. "Sh—strawberry shortcake. That's bad news if she doesn't know he's vetted. This guy may not be an issue, but she needs to watch herself."

Indeed, everything about the circumstances gave a blaring red flag, and I wondered how they hadn't waved right in her face. Hopefully, somehow, she knew about his embassy connection, though we'd need to review safety measures, just to be certain she could spot a bad actor when he showed up.

He'd let her think she came to him, but he could've marked her long before she ever showed up. He'd given himself a sad little story to elicit sympathy, plus he was new to the city, so she got to play the seasoned one despite being an American expat. He was also a decent-looking guy, attractive enough to make her comfortable but not so hand-some she'd be intimidated.

He was the perfect little honey pot for an American woman, and the fact she was a foreign government employee made it even more of a possibility he had ulterior motives. As embassy staff, she would've been briefed on this kind of thing annually, at least. Only because he was close friends with an LES did I not *actually* feel so concerned, but did she know that?

He could just be a total jerk out to do her wrong, unsuspecting woman that she is.

"That didn't seem rather coincidental?" I asked, trying not to betray that I knew he'd been vetted.

She gave me an annoyed look. "Of course it was. Do you think I just voluntarily handed over my clearance level and embassy employment to see if he's actually a bad guy? No. I was friendly, didn't say anything about what I do or even where I worked, and we parted ways. It was a full month before I saw him again and he was with a friend who works at the embassy at this café, and he waved but didn't approach me. Later, that same friend confirmed they were old pals, which tells me József must not be all that bad. If he'd had a grander scheme, it would've unfolded already, and his buddy never would've gotten the job he did."

Ah, smart woman. But I wasn't going to ease up just yet because I liked that fire in her eyes.

"You might be underestimating him."

She took a deep breath before leveling her head and

giving me a look that was so no-nonsense and straightforward, it made my heart trip.

"I appreciate your concern. With that said, I've somehow managed to live my life and function just fine without you for"—she checked her watch—"ah, that's right, *my entire life.* So while I know you have certain training and skills, I would like to say that I am not an idiot, and József is not a threat. He has never once asked me for information or even about my job other than whether I like it. I'm not over here spilling the government's secrets which, by the way, I know very few of. To top it off, thanks to both his status as a friend of an LES *and* the fact that I asked around about him at the embassy and he's known and liked, he's not a threat. But gosh, Ryan Whateveryournameis, thanks for telling me how to handle myself."

I nodded, put in my place—for now. "Fair enough. Forgive my intrusion."

She blinked as though she hadn't expected the response. "Uh, of course. Forgiven."

With a half smile, I tucked a stack of forint under the edge of her saucer, eliciting a scowl. "I'll see you soon, Em."

She chuckled softly. "See you soon, Ry."

I didn't bother to hide my full smile as I walked away, even with North's nattering and South's ridiculous exclamations over the exchange. I'd already liked Emily Wender based on our interactions in Germany, and this face-to-face had drilled it home. She was intelligent, exciting, and wasn't about to cow to me when I got a little pushy.

This assignment just got better and better.

CHAPTER FIVE

Emily

The mood at work deteriorated rapidly when the news came two days later. West and his team had been giving classes and there was a fair amount of hubbub, particularly from the female contingent who had not stopped praising how handsome and capable Ryan Jacobs and North Jones were. I suspected North's name wasn't Jones, but what did I care?

The bad news arrived when Nancy, a file clerk from the sixth-floor interior office, didn't show for a third day in a row. Her friend Sandy had gone to her house that night and banged on her door, even tried to get the building manager to let her in, but no luck. The embassy security had gone on high alert, this sinking sensation growing in all of us.

Well, at least it was for me. I couldn't say for anyone else, but having two women in the span of a few weeks disappear without a word? Not normal. And not really something that just *happened.*

Anytime I let myself feel relieved about moving back to the US and getting way from all this, a sharp stab of guilt caught me between the ribs. I shouldn't feel grateful to be leaving, should I? No. I should be trying to figure out what was happening.

"Emily, is the schedule for your symposium complete and ready for the briefing?" Lucinda stood peering at me over the edge of her tablet.

This, I will not miss. And I had no guilt about it, either.

"It is, though I'm not sure it's necessary to brief the schedule. It's not for another two months."

This was my final project and frustratingly, it'd been pushed from the original date to one after my contracted year here was up. I'd end up coming back for about a week, but since it was for this job, my new work—whatever it would end up being—would hopefully be understanding about the travel.

"We'll need extra security, and I need to be tracking the expenses, as you know." She said this without actually looking at me.

"I've submitted the budget and have finalized all of the arrangements. I have confirmation from Christensen, Khatri, Chen, and Bankoye, and I should hear from the others within the week."

Just listing those names gave me a little thrill. I'd been working to bring strong women from various industries to speak at a women's symposium here that would be open to young entrepreneurs and women in business, along with the women involved in the embassy work from Budapest and surrounding embassies. It would be a shiny gold star on the schedule, a feel-good event, and I wouldn't miss it for the world, even if I didn't love that I'd have to haul back to Europe within a month of moving stateside.

Lucinda finally gave me her acquiescence in the form of her signature impatient sigh. "Fine. Just email it all to me so I have visibility. When you disappear on us—" She cleared her throat. "Excuse me, that was uncalled for."

Her voice wavered in a rare show of emotion, enough so that I glanced at her, but she looked perfectly composed, if a bit contrite.

"What I mean is, when you leave, I will be managing the event until you return."

I nodded, feeling softer toward her now that I'd seen a glimmer of human emotion in her eyes. It'd never occurred to me she'd be affected by the women who were missing because she didn't display any emotions beyond impatience and smugness. But of course she was. She lived here year-round, and her husband often traveled for his job, so she was on her own fairly frequently.

Note to self, ease up on the judgment. It was tough on all of us to know colleagues and friends were in danger, let alone grapple with what it might mean for us or our peers. "Yes, and I greatly appreciate that. I couldn't do it without you. I'll get everything to you within the hour."

"Thank you." With that, she turned and left, padding in her sensible heels and tweed skirt like something out of an office sitcom.

Twenty minutes later, I'd sent everything I had on the event to her and though I didn't love her sticking her nose in, I would need her to keep things rolling until the event itself. I'd be out of touch while I traveled back and then likely for a few days until I had email account access established at my new job since getting my CAC access and new permissions for a new job always took a minute. I'd narrowed my options down to two—one job at Fort Liberty, one back at Fort Campbell, and I owed them both a response within the week… I just hoped I'd figure out which one was best on top of everything else.

Where will Nancy be by then?

The thought snaked through me, casting a pall over my thoughts yet again. How many more women would be missing by the time I came back for the symposium? I shuddered at the thought, dread solidifying like stones in my gut. This wasn't normal. Something must be happening, but what?

"You okay in there?" a strikingly handsome man asked through thick-framed glasses and a charming half smile.

I blinked back into the moment, having evidently spaced *entirely* out and not even heard the man knock on my door.

"Uh, yes, sorry. Are you looking for Lucinda? Our admin's on lunch, but I'm happy to help you." I stood, moved around my desk, and then stopped short when West stepped in.

"Ms. Emily Wender, please meet North Jones."

Ah. Yeah, it tracked. This man was gorgeous in a similar way as West. He was clearly muscular under his suit, had facial hair separating him from our dear sweet Marine guards, and had a confidence that said he could get stuff done.

"Great to meet you, Ms. Wender." He extended his hand, and I took it.

"Can I help you? I guess you're between briefings?" Or classes? They were being called counterintelligence briefings for some and workshops for others, depending on who was attending.

"Just checking in since we had a spare moment." West's eyes swept over my office and landed back on me. "I hope you're doing well."

Something about the way he was looking at me made my chest pinch, almost like he really did hope so—like he knew the news was upsetting. And I wondered if he knew anything about what was really going on.

"Thank you. Do you... is there any chance you guys have insight on the situation here? What's happening?"

West exhaled softly. "I wish I could say I did. Unfortunately, no. That's one reason we're here—trying to make sure everyone remembers the basics and protocols so we minimize the potential for any more disappearances."

"Was Ms. Akers a friend of yours?" North asked, his dark brows arching with concern.

"We were friendly. She was closest to Sandy Gordon since they worked together. It's just generally very upsetting. I mean, what are the odds they find them?"

Nancy and Janie, and who knew how many other women, had been abducted. Maybe that wasn't the right term, but at this point, I wasn't going to pretend they'd magically returned stateside without a word to anyone just to ease my own mind.

West's gorgeous blue eyes found mine and pinned me in place. "I can promise you that whoever is looking for them won't stop until they find them."

And though he'd said he didn't know anything, this response—the vehemence in his voice and the hard edge to his promise—they told me he knew they wouldn't stop.

That maybe, what he actually meant was *he* wouldn't stop.

It was all the wrong time and wrong place for the thought, but it arrived unbidden anyway. I was glad he was here, glad he'd be the one helping, because I believed every word and it eased some of my worry just a little to think of these two personally working to get them back.

CHAPTER SIX

North snapped photos discreetly as we wandered through the offices and stopped to chat with embassy employees.

"Everything's coming through clear. Good work."

East's feedback about the photo clarity was a relief. We wouldn't be able to get away with this during work hours more than once, and while he was fully capable of hacking the video feeds of the CCTVs around the embassy, it could cause problems we didn't want to start if we could help it.

This way, we got to meet all the staff, even the ones who didn't bother showing up for our security briefings, and we could also check out the personal dynamics and offices of just about everyone. Even the ambassador was in today, which meant almost everyone else would be, too.

"It's nice you guys could come out and do this. Remind the ladies to watch their backs and all."

Greg Gordon, husband to Sandy, the woman who'd raised the alarm about Nancy going missing, slapped North on the back, and I nearly coughed when I saw the irritated look on North's face, but I held it in.

"We want everyone to be cautious and smart, now and in the future. On that note, do you personally have any concerns?" Something made me want to press on this guy a little, and I rarely ignored those little somethings.

"Me? Concerns? Well, I wonder if maybe the women should have a curfew? Or they should be walked home by their husbands and such. But otherwise..."

"He means anything personally. One thing we review in the course is addressing personal areas that are exploitable. Obviously, everyone is routinely vetted for security clearances, but they can be simpler things." North gave him a smile like *we're all friends here* and nodded at the watch on Gordon's wrist. "Looks like the career trajectory's going okay."

Gordon chuckled. "Well, yes. I'm very pleased to be here, even if it means government pay. And this? Honestly, it's a hand-me-down. But the wife and I keep it simple here, and we're both working. No kids. We do just fine for ourselves. Thank you for checking, of course, since I know this is all part of keeping everyone safe."

Seemed a bit odd to thank someone for asking if they'd incurred debt to buy their Rolex on a government salary, but of course this man, a cog in the diplomatic wheel, wasn't about to delve into his personal debts with us. We didn't have such authority—at least not for our cover. In reality, we had authorization from the Secretary of Defense to get our job done, and we would. Like the good mini diplomat he was, he was going to schmooze.

Someone in this embassy was hiding something. Knew

something. Had let slip something. And women were missing because of it.

More than that, we suspected secrets, maybe weapons, and a lot more, were going missing, too.

Maksim Volkov was the man who most likely sat at the helm of this, and we needed to know who had gotten mixed up with him. We'd infiltrated his compound last year with the help of Eddie James and Bri Williamson. He'd discovered Eddie was a spy, though she'd managed to convince Volkov, or so we currently believed, that she had used Williamson. Because of this, the Cardinals—aka me and my team, the four of us—weren't on his naughty list since we'd posed as Williamson's entourage.

We needed to stop the leak here. Working from the embassy end of the thread would be our best bet for finding any leads connecting Volkov to this mess. It would also help recover Nancy and Janie and with starting to close up the information pipeline to the criminal organizations.

"Thanks for talking with us. Please pass along our sympathies to your wife. I'm sure it's been hard on her with her friend missing." North smiled his charming little smile and the guy visibly relaxed.

Sure, some people weren't comfortable small talking with strangers, but as a mid-ranking foreign official, he must be familiar and relatively comfortable with meeting new people. And he'd quickly risen to the top of my suspicions list.

We chatted with a few more people, perused any part of the building we could see without being too obvious to anyone watching, and finally exited. By the time we left her floor, Emily wasn't in her office, and I ignored the comments North made in an attempt to rile me up about missing her.

I'd just seen her. I was working. I shouldn't have been thinking about her this much as it was.

Though no small part of me had sighed in relief when East's very thorough background check last night had come up clean. Nothing suspicious about her whatsoever, and all the details of her life painted an even more appealing picture of the woman.

She was independent, successful, and clearly well-liked in her professional circles. She was leaving her one-year position in Budapest in a few weeks with what appeared to be rave reviews at her back and had a few prospects for work in the States, but East hadn't seen any specifics there. She had strong connections with several military spouses who appeared to be her close friends, though she didn't appear to have a history dating anyone seriously.

Hmm. Granted, East's information didn't say that as much as "No romantic links" and even in that case, I wasn't sad to hear it.

The only issue was József. And sure... maybe he really was just a nice friend. Unfortunately, in my life, I'd learned there were genuinely bad people out there. Maybe they hadn't started out that way, but life, circumstances, cultural expectations—whatever. Those things could shape a person, and then all that's left is the choices they make. I'd seen too many examples of people making evil choices to have a sunny disposition or to believe in coincidence.

"Dreaming about chocolate brown eyes gazing into yours?" South said as we entered the safe house a few minutes later.

We'd hunkered down in a part of the city not far from where most embassy employees lived. Our safehouse was outfitted with every manner of signal disrupter and functioned as securely as a top secret building in the US save for a few layers we couldn't supply internationally. Soundproof and windowless, with padded walls like a true debriefing room should be, it nestled into the larger home we rented. Our advance team came in and set these up when we didn't have them already established, though our Hungary location had been in place for a while.

"Don't harass him or he'll just freeze you out. Ask me how I know."

I didn't need to look at North to see the wide-eyed look he'd no doubt be sharing with South. I'd known these men for a solid decade, and we'd worked a small-ops team for five and on a larger team for longer. I knew them almost as well as I knew myself.

"I'm happy for you to tease me about whatever you idiots want when we're done with this mission and we have the missing women back. Until then—"

"Oh, oh, oh. I see how it is. Going to go all noble on us so we feel guilty. But wasn't it you two days ago who nearly blew your cover in front of someone just to talk to the woman? Where was your nobility and mission focus then?" North waited with hands on hips.

I sighed and sifted through the many responses I wanted to fling at him in search of the one that would shut this all up. Yes, I was drawn to Emily. No, nothing could happen. *Maybe, if we meet again...*

Even my own mind was against me. Logically, the odds of us running into each other here had been fairly slim, all things considered. It happening again when I wasn't on mission and could actually do something to spend more time with her? Defeatingly slim.

"Enough. I've got a lead."

East's gruff voice cut through the snickers and jabs still

coming from North and South, and we all snapped to attention.

"Let's hear it," I said, signaling we were all ready. No more nonsense and teasing. If we had actionable intel, even one small piece, it could be the hairpin to help us jimmy the lock on this whole situation.

And after East showed us what he'd found based on the snapshots North's camera had sent back, after hours of researching the inkling East had about where this all took us, we had a mission to propose to the Colonel and a strict timeline to execute before the window closed.

No more thoughts about Emily. There was a reason I'd avoided romantic entanglements for years, and even though she was markedly different from anyone I'd met yet, it was enough now.

Time to get to work.

CHAPTER SEVEN

Emily

Two weeks after the last time I saw West, I could've sworn someone was following me as I picked up my take-out order from my favorite restaurant near my apartment. I'd worked late, as I'd gotten in the habit of doing in order to complete everything I needed to before I left. Time was flying by now that West and his team of babes—okay, I'd only met the one, but he was absolutely at home in that category and I was going to allow my little fantasy of the rest of his team, whoever they were, to be right along with him—had left without a goodbye.

Their last few workshops and briefings had been full, especially after they'd spent the afternoon wandering the halls and talking with people. It'd taken me an entire half hour to rediscover my ability to focus and actually accomplish something. Having that man in my space...

It made me want things, okay? I couldn't explain why

this bothered me other than the fact that now, he'd left without a word, and I had the strong feeling I wouldn't see him again. Maybe ever, at this point.

Why was I so preoccupied with him anyway, especially when he pulled the disappearing act so deftly? Granted, that was part of his job, and acknowledging it only forced me to further concede he appeared to be very good at what he did, which then piled onto the massively growing list of things I liked about him, but... why? Why him? I'd looked countless handsome soldiers in the face and found my heart unmoved, but him?

It came back to the smarts and the manners paired with what I'd now discovered was a maddening swaggery confidence that bordered on cocky but fell short of it when he did things like apologize when he was wrong or show concern for people. It was all so... disarming.

I didn't love the idea of this odd longing tugging at me for the next few weeks and bleeding into my transition into a new job. With West gone, I'd finally made the call about which job to take, and I had hope it'd be a good transition. I'd been tempted to return to the education center life since I'd spent the vast majority of my time as a government employee working for ed centers on Army posts, but this new option would be another broadening effort, just like the time here in Hungary.

That nagging sensation tickled the back of my neck again, and I glanced behind me. Only a few other people bustling along, no one visibly watching me. My pace picked up and I moved faster, shy of a jog, but I was power walking in these heels despite the cobblestones in this part of the city.

Right when I entered the narrow alleyway leading to my building's door, my heart rate spiked, fear edging out all attempts at reason, and I skittered toward the door. A hand grasped my arm and I nearly shrieked until I heard his voice.

"You're okay, Emily. It's me."

Ryan freaking West.

I sucked in a relieved breath, then swung my purse at him as adrenaline and a spark of rage hit. "Are you kidding me? Why would you sneak up on me? Why—"

He pressed a hand to my mouth, and his other hand found my waist under my coat. I swallowed my words and inhaled. He'd left me plenty of room to breathe, but the intensity in his eyes as he paced me backward and pressed me just a little less than gently into the freezing brick wall made my heart flutter.

His warm palm still covered my mouth for another second until he seemed certain I wouldn't keep talking, and then he let it fall away. My breath rushed out, a thin white cloud in the chill evening air.

His gaze didn't waver, though. He spoke in a tone so quiet, I would've bet money someone standing a few feet away wouldn't have been able to make out his words.

"I shouldn't have come. But we're heading back, and I wanted to see you."

My mouth dropped open. *Oh.* So. Not so disappeary. "To see me."

He only stared, and his intensity made all kinds of things happen inside me. My stomach tightened and my knees went loose. Everything heightened as he exhaled and his hand flexed at my waist.

The cold of the wall began seeping through the wool of my coat, but he radiated heat in front of me.

My breath came quick and shallow, and I had the weirdest impulse telling me to lean in and kiss him.

Okay, not exactly *weirdest* considering how much I'd thought about this man over the last few years and how much more I liked him, even after his pushiness about József and then his disappearing act the last two weeks.

"Yes. We've been occupied for a bit. And now we're heading back."

To the States. To North Carolina? I hadn't confirmed he was in the EMU, but he had to be. He just had to be, with the whole covert mission and all, not to mention his hair was longer than most soldiers and he had facial hair. In the US, only special operations and special forces had this kind of leeway.

"And so you're here... to see me." My heart fluttered and I wondered... what exactly did he expect to get from me?

And maybe more importantly, what did *I* want from him?

He better not be some guy who thought he was about to see the inside of my bedroom based on blazing chemistry and my apparently obvious singlehood—

"Just to say goodbye." His words came in that same low, deep voice.

I shivered at the same time disappointment drowned the butterflies in my chest. And now that I knew he wasn't here for some kind of last-minute fling, I felt a loss. Was he really just going to go?

"Can you... come up for dinner? I have enough to share, I'm sure."

He dipped his head and his jaw flexed. "Wish I could."

And with this, he took my chin in his fingers and tilted my head a few degrees, then pressed his lips to my cheek, his short beard rasping against my skin, then another, slower kiss to the corner of my mouth.

My breath rushed out and lips parted as he pulled away,

but then he came in for another soft, slow press just shy of my actual mouth. Like he had all the time in the world and all the patience I definitely didn't have.

My scrambled mind caught up a second too late. I turned my face more purposefully, eager to share this moment with him if it was all we'd have, but he stepped away, a chilly draft rushing in between us.

"Bye for now, Em."

I watched him turn and walk and whispered an ineffectual, "See ya, Ry."

An instant later, I'd moved into the building and plodded up the stairs, all the while marveling at the fact that I'd never managed to tell him I, too, would be heading stateside soon. And not just stateside, but to North Carolina, likely to the very military base where he worked.

CHAPTER EIGHT

Emily

A few weeks later and after enduring the utterly draining first part of my international move, I walked into a restaurant in downtown Southern Pines, North Carolina, with a sense of surrealism clinging to every detail.

First, the spring day felt hot and stuffy, but inside the gastropub, the AC made it feel frigid. Adjusting back to such intense air conditioning would take a minute. The embassy had had it, but the building was old and they just didn't air condition things in Europe like they did in the US.

Note to self: always bring a sweater. Wherever. Forever.

And second, I couldn't believe the day I'd had. I couldn't even blame it on jet lag. I'd powered through the worst of it my first few days back and was feeling generally fine.

No, it really hadn't been anything to do with me.

"Hey! Oh my gosh, you're here!" Katie Miller slid out of the booth behind a smiling, adorable Noah, her soldier husband, and she hugged me tight.

These two were precious. I'd gotten to know Katie when she moved to Germany to be with Noah after having been married and living separately for over five years. Their story slowly unfolded as we'd gotten to know her—they'd married to get her out of a horrible situation. They'd lived apart until Noah was taken captive on a deployment and seriously injured, at which point the Army called her to come to the military hospital and be with him. It all made sense, except the part where they'd been married in name only. But then circumstances forced them to own up to their mutual pining and a future they wanted together and here they were.

"Hey yourself, friend. So good to see you."

She looked fantastic—maybe that was the glow of marriage to a man who was willing to do anything for you and having his baby. Or... babies?

She must've seen my eyes slip over her typically slender frame. "Yeah. Number two's due in the summer."

I laughed and pulled her to me again. "Why didn't you tell me? Who else knows?"

We had a monthly online video chat to catch up with Bec Jones, Livie Wolfe, Summer Masters, Ariel Reynolds, and the two of us—our old Kugelfels crew—but I'd missed last month's and no one had said a word about this little package.

"No one, actually. I wanted to wait until you got here and I saw you in real life because how often do I get to tell my closest friends anything in person?" She beamed.

I shook my head and my throat grew tight. She was absolutely radiant. She had the kind of beauty you'd notice anyway, but like this? Just stunning. "I'm so, so happy for you. For both of you."

"Thanks. We're obviously pretty happy about it."

"And sweet Leah?"

Noah chuckled. "She has no idea what's coming."

We laughed together at the one-year-old's fate of sharing the spotlight, and I resisted the urge to rub at the space over my heart. I ached because of the day, the move, the change. This was all just... good.

"How was your first day?" Katie asked, straightening a menu on the table in front of her as we sat down.

"Let's see. I arrived to find my boss had been relieved and no one else even knew I was coming."

Katie's mouth dropped open and Noah's eyes widened.

"Exactly. Then I found out that my position no longer exists. Apparently, my boss hired me with full knowledge the position was transitioning away from GS to contract."

I couldn't even summon anger about it. It seemed too ridiculous to be believed, frankly, so I'd basically just kept moving instead of letting it sink in.

"Wait, what? How is that even possible? You did all the stuff. You accepted the position formally, right?"

I nodded. It'd taken me longer than they'd wanted, but why bother hiring in the first place if the position was changing anyway?

"That's messed up," Noah said.

"Just a little," I said, then sighed loudly. "But the good news is I've now set a record for myself for shortest duration in a job by like, eleven months and twenty-six days or something, so there's that." I raised my water glass in a sarcastic toast.

Katie made a face. "I'm so sorry. That's just... I can't even—"

"Sorry to interrupt, guys, but I had to come over."

My eyes shot up at the man's voice, and sure enough, I *did* recognize it. "Rob! I didn't realize you were at Liberty!"

I jumped out of my seat and wrapped my arms around his neck right when his wrapped around my waist.

"How are you, kid? You look great." He grinned and shook his head like he couldn't believe what he was seeing.

"Aren't you several years younger than me or something?"

Rob Waverly was the quintessential flirt. He'd been a good friend in Germany. In fact, I recalled seeing him chat with West during the time he'd been at Kugelfels. For some reason, I had a vivid memory of Rob and West talking quietly in the parking lot of the ed center... and why was I thinking about West right now? Why did *everything* lately turn my mind over to that man?

"Nah. Not possible. You're not a day over thirty, are you?" He winked, then leaned in to press a kiss to my cheek. "Seriously, though, is this a secret Kugelfels reunion and I wasn't invited?"

Noah and Katie had stood again, and Rob shook Noah's hand before leaning in for a hug. They'd been through a lot together, but it didn't seem like they'd seen each other in a while.

"It's been too long. How's the baby?" Rob asked, sliding in to kiss Katie's cheek.

"She's big. And she's going to be a big sister." Noah's smile lit up the back half of the room, and Rob met it with another hearty handshake and a blinding smile of his own.

"We need more Millers on this earth, so good on you."

Noah chuckled at that. "Just doing our part."

Katie's blush reminded me how quiet she'd been. She

wasn't shy with me anymore, but I wondered if she'd had a hard time meeting people here.

We all sat down, and Rob slid in next to me. "I'm not trying to crash, but I'm nosy and I could swear I heard you say you're jobless? Is that right?"

I sighed, exaggerating my sense of defeat. Honestly, I felt very little other than disbelief. I hadn't even let myself think about next steps beyond hopping onto USAJobs again and searching like my ability to pay my rent depended on it.

Hilariously, it kinda did. And the process to get hired usually took months.

"I'm not trying to razz you, I'm genuinely asking. I swear, it's meant to be that we're all here, because I actually just sat through a meeting talking about a GS job they're trying to quick-fill at my work and I think you'd be perfect for it."

"What's the job?" I couldn't pretend I wasn't interested, and being in this world long enough had taught me never to say no to more information.

"It's a kind of family member morale type job? I wasn't fully tuned in, I admit, but I will figure out if it might work and e-mail you details, yeah?"

He glanced up and notched his chin up, acknowledging someone across the room. I followed the line of sight and saw a group of men sliding onto barstools.

He was so casual and confident, so nonchalant about this thing that could be my next step. Rob was a fellow *be here now* buddy, but I could've stood for him to roll out a bit more for me here. That said, I wasn't going to fault him for not knowing details of a job that had nothing to do with him. In the end, it wasn't likely to be a fit, but he was a dear to even mention it.

"I've got to get going, but seriously, Wender, I'm going

to call you. This could be good, especially if you're done being fancy at an embassy and you don't want Ed anymore."

I'd left education in Germany and hadn't minded the actual work of my job in Hungary. Back here, I really was up for continuing to climb the ladder in a different avenue, as long as it sounded interesting. "I'm open. I mostly want the paycheck. But wait, where is the job?"

He'd been shaking Noah's hand again and smiling at Katie, busy getting out of the booth.

"It's in USASOC—Special Operations Command. Could be an interesting time for you," he said. "Plus then, you'll get to see me all the time."

With one last wink, he jogged to meet up with his friends, and we all grinned after him, as was so often the effect when faced with the man.

Disbelief and excitement and no small amount of amazement filled me. "Did Rob Waverly really just offer me a job in special operations?"

CHAPTER NINE

I shook the colonel's hand as he congratulated the team.

"Well done. It'll be a while before Maksim Volkov rebuilds that leg of his little empire, thanks to you." Colonel Patch gave North a slap on the back when he released my hand, awarding us each a few seconds of eye contact to show he really meant it.

Some commanders didn't even bother. They treated the teams like it was all in a day's work. And sure, slipping into a US Embassy undetected and performing a complex security check without anyone noticing, then maintaining cover while actually teaching security measures to the staff and ferreting out any intel we could, then acting on that intel to find two missing US citizens and shut down the pipeline of weapons leading to the biggest arms proliferation in Eastern Europe since the war in Bosnia was technically a few days' work.

From the time we entered the embassy to the time we recovered the women and handed over several other international citizens to the international task force, rerouted arms shipments, caught the middle man, and set a liiiiittle fire that took out the warehouse where a big cache had been stored a few hours from downtown Budapest, it'd been just shy of a month.

We'd planned that op for weeks before we'd arrived in country and then tracked a few people we'd identified as part of Volkov's organization. We'd been waiting on a reason to move, some sign that we could break into the pipeline.

When the first embassy employee disappeared, it piqued our interest, and we pushed our timeline so we had a clear reason to be at the embassy and check things out for ourselves. The hope had been to ferret out who was leaking information, and being there when the second woman was taken gave us plenty of reason to act in the eyes of the DoD.

All of it lined up with the unit's mission, and no part was particularly standout in comparison to what any other team had done recently. Even so, Patch didn't make it seem like what we did was nothing.

His method of reward was old school—kudos and handshakes, backslaps and attaboys, and then of course, the eye contact. If he weren't so dang genuine, it'd be laughable, but we always walked away from AARs with him feeling good.

Even if things hadn't gone perfectly.

I'd reported the run-in with Emily on the first night itself, as well as our interactions afterward. If she'd tipped anyone off that we weren't who our cover said we were, we could've been seriously derailed. And would it matter much after the fact? No. Not really. She couldn't prove where I actually worked, and in the end, we had actionable intel to get in there and for what we'd done after. Department of Defense would look the other way.

But State? *Yeah.* State wouldn't be too thrilled, especially when they already had their spooks looking into other issues at the embassy. Granted, we'd just had a very successful joint operation with one of State's super squads, Kappa Sector, including one that led to us having the intel we needed for our recent successful op, so they shouldn't be complaining too much.

Could US soldiers like us enter an embassy? Absolutely. Could they enter and look around and take stuff without asking? Hard no. Not without red tape covering miles, and definitely not without tipping off whatever jackhole was leaking key info to the bad guys.

And trust this guy, Maksim Volkov, was one bad man. Weapons smuggling was but one of his hobbies. He also had fingers in several other bad guy pies, like drug running, human trafficking, and the one to have gotten Uncle Sam's attention: brokering the sales of government secrets.

Neat little portfolio, right? Long story short, we'd cut Volkov off at the knees for now, at least in one part of Eastern Europe. No weapons sales now that we'd literally destroyed his stash, a whole lot less cash because of it, and hopefully drying up the well of intel from the leak at the embassy, assuming we did in fact get the right guy. Greg Gordon didn't seem all that desperate when we saw him interrogated by our buddies at State, but we'd tipped them off and they'd found more than enough incriminating evidence to put him away for treason for a lifetime. That feeling North and I both got from him when we'd talked on our little meet and greet a few weeks back had been right on.

That said, it wasn't settled. I couldn't put a name to it,

and I'd mentioned it to the guys. They'd agreed, but we couldn't figure out what felt unfinished. Too easy, maybe, not that it had been particularly easy. We'd need to circle back in a few weeks once the dust settled and confirm no one had tried to fill in the gap we'd created, but it felt like more than that somehow.

"You thinking Volkov will recover from the gravy train being cut off with his other income streams?" North asked the CO.

"We'll need to follow up, but you can get started on that next week. I'm sure your squadron will be working on it. State'll have eyes on anyone they can find in the meantime. At least we got the women back, and hopefully, Volkov's people will be distracted enough they won't worry about grabbing anyone else. I'd say we're good for a minute, so enjoy the long weekend." He gave us one last nod, then exited and disappeared down the hallway.

"I always feel like I should say something when he does that. The intense eye contact thing. Like... thank you? Is that weird? But then it *is* weird because he's so intense and sincere about it, and he's the one thanking us. After Schlock, I don't know if I'll ever get used to Patch." North shook his head, gazing almost dreamily after Colonel Patch.

"Schlock was forking garbage. He's to blame for half of the cra—b apples we're cleaning up now," South grumped.

"I've got to check in with Jimmy and then I'm out. We doing dinner tomorrow?" I asked.

They mumbled agreements on their way to the team room. I headed the other way, back to give my squadron commanding officer a quick debrief of the kudos meeting we'd just had with Patch. Though the teams operated internationally with a fair amount of autonomy, everything we did to train and prepare went through the unit as a whole and our squadron at a smaller level. On bigger ops, we had the commander on-site to assist and literally make decisions when we dealt with high value targets or more nuanced situations.

Jimmy leaned against the doorframe to his office, chatting with a small group. When I caught his eye, he said, "Thanks, guys. Have a good weekend" and turned into his office.

I followed and waited for what he needed to say.

"Had to check something real quick before you head out. Can you confirm the civilian's name from last month?"

He leaned back, arms crossed over his chest, and the angle was just past comfortable. He'd broken the chair one afternoon when his wife had called to tell him she'd cheated on him and now wanted a divorce—great way to let a guy know. Jimmy was levelheaded but that threw him and the chair had suffered for it.

Even with all this, thinking about Emily made my pulse tick up ever so slightly. "Emily Wender. I missed it on the sweep of employees before the op." I didn't recall even seeing her name, and it would've stuck out to me.

"I thought that was it, which is why I was startled to have Rob Waverly waltz in here and introduce his friend Emily Wender not thirty minutes ago."

Only years of training to respond slowly, calmly, kept me from jumping out of my seat and raving, "Where?! Where?!"

"Really? Why's Rob taking her around?"

One of Jimmy's eyebrows lifted like he suspected something, but he only said, "They're old friends, apparently. He connected her with the hiring committee a few weeks back, and today sounds like he offered to wrap up the tour after her last in-processing brief this morning."

He got her a job? I supposed it made sense they knew each other. Rob had been stationed at Kugelfels when I'd met Emily—in fact, I'd led the rescue mission that snatched him and Noah Miller from a quaint little dungeon in the Kandahar province a few years back. I'd never heard Rob talk about her, but why would he? We were in different squadrons, didn't work together all that much. We were friendly in that I'd had a hand in saving his life—and his hand, for that matter—and as he'd once told me, those events were what pushed him to work toward getting selected as an operator officer for EMU.

There'd be no reason for him to mention Emily. He had no idea I knew her. Or, rather, had met her.

Or more accurately, had been thinking about her since I'd met her in Germany and now couldn't get her out of my head despite knowing I should stop being an idiot.

"Seems highly coincidental that she's here after being there," Jimmy said, interrupting my ridiculous off-kilter thoughts.

"You reading something into that?" I asked, knowing how none of us like coincidences.

"Nah, not like that. Just, since you knew her there and now she's here, you might want to go track her down and say hi. I'm guessing she doesn't know you work here..."

I shook my head. "No. Not specifically, anyway. She knew I was working, but no one knows EMU even exists, right?"

He snorted at the old joke and waved me off. "Course not. No one's ever heard of us."

Pretty much everyone knew EMU existed, just like they'd known about Delta Force. But after a point, the news had become so saturated with discussion of Delta, they'd changed the name. We were still technically assigned to

First Special Forces Detachment-Delta. But that wouldn't be written down anywhere on a person's file anyway, so instead, we were the mysterious, nebulous Exceptional Mission Unit. Leadership liked to act like no one knew we existed—not in any form. So it'd become a joke—that the only people who don't talk about EMU is EMU. Everyone else sure didn't mind.

"Have a good weekend. We're getting drinks tomorrow if you want to join us," I offered, knowing he wouldn't. He waved me off as I exited his office and glanced around.

I had a ton to do before I left, but first things first. There was a question I needed answered. In my gut, I already knew, but I had to confirm it.

Would I react to her the way I had every other time I'd seen her? Would the heat and connection be there just as quickly here on American soil when there was no rush, no ticking clock to force my interest or her attention? I'd just have to see.

That last goodbye in Budapest had been just that—one last glimpse. One last stolen moment. I hadn't imagined having her so close, let alone accessible to me without a time limit. I'd even kept myself from claiming her lips like I'd desperately wanted simply because I suspected one kiss would leave me wanting her indefinitely.

Not that stopping short of it had prevented the same fate.

And now that we'd sewn up the Volkov nonsense well enough, could I relax into letting her become a reality, if she wanted this, instead of just an unattainable dream version of life?

We'd have to answer the first things first.

If Emily Wender was in the building, I'd find her.

CHAPTER TEN

Emily

Rob grinned as his squadron commander retreated to his office, and I turned to face him, still experiencing more than a little disbelief that he worked for the EMU, and he'd gotten me a job here.

Have I mentioned how much I love spy stuff? Have I ever talked about how *Alias* is my favorite show or how I gobbled up the fictionalized story of the Delta Force in *The Unit* years ago?

I may not date soldiers as a rule, but something about being in a building full of the literal best soldiers in the *world* was more than a little thrilling. Working with people who were amazing at what they did was the absolute best.

I'd been overwhelmed, excited, and a little worried I was in over my head when I nervously drove onto the compound for my first day of training earlier this week. But I'd already gotten a feel for the place and saw room for ideas and what I could bring to the table. I'd been brainstorming like mad as I'd submitted resumes and interviewed in what had been a whirlwind two weeks.

"You seem happy. Are you happy?"

Rob's smile hadn't wavered. He was absolutely a little ball of badass soldier sunshine and clearly got a kick out of being the one to get me in the door.

"I think so? I'm mostly over here feeling like this is all some crazy dream orchestrated by J. J. Abrams, and I don't wanna wake up."

He chuckled. "Nah, not a dream. But I get the feeling. It's pretty unique to get to be here, to work with these people. We're talking about the unit that brought down some of the world's biggest terrorists. Who've rescued kidnapped Americans and—"

"Really? I didn't know that was part of what you guys do." Though I'd heard both Nancy and Janie had been found alive, and I'd wondered if West... rather, if EMU had had anything to do with it.

"Yes, we do. But obviously, we're not giving interviews afterward. Oftentimes, the fact that the person is missing doesn't hit the news in the first place—when the entities keeping intel bleed to a minimum work effectively. A media circus doesn't do much for us except sometimes in the case when a regime has someone high-profile, or we can use public opinion to drive a change in policy. Those are above our heads and not the ones we worry about. Mostly it's nuns and idiots."

I blinked at him, and my shock played over my face. He laughed loudly, the same free laugh I'd enjoyed years ago. My heart warmed, happy to be reunited with this friend in the midst of a challenging transition.

He explained himself. "Two totally separate categories. Nuns who are working at aid camps or missionaries are one category. They end up in places where some criminal gets a visit from the good idea fairy, and there we have ourselves a mission. And alternately, idiots, usually tourists thinking they can do or go somewhere because they are wealthy Americans and should get to do what they want, even when State tells them not to. Those are always fun, too."

"Ah, gotcha. Have you done a lot of that... kind of thing?" Maybe not an entirely appropriate question, now that it'd jumped out of my mouth.

"As you can imagine, you're not going to get all the details on what we do. You'll be missing clearance for more than knowing the basics here."

I made a face and his eyes twinkled back at me, so I nudged him away with my elbow. "Rude. But also, I get it. We're need to know here, for reals."

He raised his brows. "Legit."

I grinned at him. "So? What now?"

His eyes shifted past me, and he did what I was discovering was Unit standard greeting, a chin lift toward someone coming down the hallway. "Meet my buddy, West."

Lightning shot through me and I turned in slow motion. *This is happening.* I'd wondered if he would be here, but in the whirlwind of onboarding and learning the ropes here, I'd honestly been so focused on, well, right here and now, I'd forgotten this might happen.

Probably for the best because in the seconds since I'd heard his name, nerves had buzzed through me from my belly out to my fingers and toes, and my mind was doing something like a hysterical boyband scream-cry of excitement while my other non-lizard brain was trying to remind me I was a professional adult woman who was *not* going to act like an idiot in front of this man.

There he stood, dressed just like every other guy I'd seen today, in a plaid shirt with sleeves rolled at the wrists and dark utility pants. He had that typical settled look about him, like he'd been born comfortable in his skin and never had a second of doubt about anything.

Must be nice.

Honestly, I'd kept an eye out for him. The more I saw of this place, the more convinced I became that Ryan West worked here and he'd had a mission at the embassy those weeks before I left. I knew he and his team had been up to something, and he'd admitted as much when we'd had our little meeting, but he never confirmed he worked here. I'd known it in my gut, but the confirmation launched a thrill to my toes.

Well, that and maybe just being near him, setting eyes on him again. I hadn't managed to banish the memory of his soft, slow kisses before he'd left. I hadn't gotten over the fact that right when I'd assumed he'd disappeared again, he'd shown up specifically to say goodbye.

What did that even mean? He hadn't quite kissed me on the lips, and oh, how I'd wanted him to. He'd seemed to want it, too, but stopped short of it quite purposefully.

Okay, but seriously, I'd been over this until I was sick of it and tried to remind myself I might not *ever* see him again, let alone anytime soon. It'd almost felt like a break up, watching him walk away and knowing that might be all we ever got. I'd promised myself I'd stay focused and not keep my eyes flitting down the hallway, waiting to catch a glimpse of him around the corner and have him reappear in my life. Of course, it was nearly impossible to avoid thinking of him as I'd interviewed and then in-processed here. And now...

"Emily and I have met," he told Rob, sending an untimely flush to my chest and cheeks. *Untimely but not unexpected.*

Rob made no secret of his delight at this. "You have? Where'd you guys meet?"

"She—"

"He—"

Our gazes snagged as we both stopped. One of West's thick brows arched. My stomach practiced cartwheels.

Clearing my throat, I tried again. "He came into the ed center at Kugelfels."

"Of course, that makes sense. I mean, not that he'd test there, but that you would've met there. That's where I met you both, too." Rob made a cheesy little *uh-oh* face. "Well actually, I guess I met you in Afghanistan, huh?"

West patted his back. He had a few years on Rob for sure, but hard to tell how many. Rob's whole energy was just more of that Golden Retriever youth and West had this... how to describe it? Something more like Eric Wolfe had had. Or Nick Masters. Men who'd traveled a road, lived life, and would only tell you about it if prodded over a glass of fine whiskey.

Rob would flop right down out of nowhere and offer you a job. Invite you to a barbecue the next day at his friend's house. Ask if you needed help moving in.

West would back you up into a freezing brick wall and light you on fire, then almost kiss you, and say goodbye like he meant it and like you'd lost something.

Or, you know, something like that.

"So you're giving an orientation tour?" West asked, eyes dropping to me before ticking back up to Rob.

Rob started walking down the hallway, and West and I moved with him.

"Yep. I took over from the chaplain. She just needs to do her updated CAC access and then her zero day is done." He held up a hand to me for a high five and proved my internal point well.

"Sure enough. Thanks for taking me through. And more than that, thanks for setting all of this in motion. You went above and beyond."

Rob beamed. "Right place, right time. Come 'ere."

He pulled me into a hug, then stepped back and lifted his chin to the office at my right. "This is where you'll gussy up your CAC so you're all set to actually work next week."

"Perfect. Thank you, again." I absolutely felt West's eyes on me, but I didn't let my own stray toward him. *Eyes on the puppy, Wender. Ignore the wolf in normal man clothing.*

"Am I seeing you this weekend?" Rob asked, already inching away like he was running late. He'd mentioned earlier he had a date tonight, and I wasn't going to fault the guy for wanting to get going and meet the lucky girl.

"TBD, if that's okay?"

"Always. Text me. If not tomorrow, maybe in a few weeks when I'm back from this trip?"

"Sounds good. Be safe!"

He grinned, then shot a "See ya, West!" over his shoulder as he jogged the other way.

I wasn't about to stand here and fumble around in front of this man who had given me the hottest little almost-kisses of my life and then left *again,* and I could tell the way my brain felt like all thumbs it wouldn't go well if I attempted conversation. What would I even say?

So, West. Remember the time you almost *kissed my*

mouth and then said goodbye? Remember how you made zero attempt to contact me after we met and so I assumed you had no interest in me and then you followed that up by being mildly possessive and kissing my almost-mouth? Me, too!

Yeah, no thanks.

Instead, I stayed focused on my job like a good little me and said, "Good to see you. I've got to get in here." Then I slipped inside the ID office, safe from the intensity crowding the air between us.

And Ryan West? If he did say something, I didn't hear it.

Rob wasn't quite right about my only needing a new Common Access Card. I had even more paperwork to fill out and got to chatting with the woman assisting me. By the time I exited the rather impressive-looking brick building, it'd been an hour, and it'd been four since I'd first entered.

I'd walked in earlier this week knowing very little, and I was walking out today, after briefings and signing NDAs and all kinds of other personnel paperwork, feeling simultaneously thrilled, anxious, and exhausted.

I wished my stuff was here and I could go home to a comfortable couch in a house I owned, but I hadn't had much luck house hunting since my life had launched into the unexpected hiring process instead of just sliding into the job I'd planned on. I'd lived in a furnished flat in Budapest, and all but a few décor items and some of my cookware had been rented. I'd shipped back most of my belongings from

Germany over a year ago, and the logistics of getting them here were irrelevant until I had a home address for delivery.

I'd feel better when I could get fully settled in. That time was coming, even if it felt far off. At least I liked my job after the wild, unexpected ride of getting here.

I exhaled, relieved to have been in the building and wishing it weren't a long weekend for everyone. I could've really gone for a few ten-hour workdays to distract me from the current flux of my life.

Though realistically, I had plenty of non-work work to do. Namely, finding a house.

I tapped the unlock button on my rental and startled when I looked up to see West sitting on the hood of the tiny car.

"Uh. Hello." Because what else did one say to a man I'd had on my mind far too much lately and who made my pulse spike just thinking about him, let alone seeing him in real life.

I didn't understand how, but the man had swagger just sitting there. He was pulling all the James Dean bad-boy vibes with his laid-back posture, and yet there was a distinct sense that he could be anywhere and he'd chosen to be right here. Waiting for me. On my car.

I mean honestly, on my car? What world is this?

"Hi."

"How did you know this was my car?" The lot had thinned considerably since I'd arrived hours ago, but there were still probably twenty cars within view.

He'd pulled a hat low over his eyes, and somehow, this made him even more attractive. Don't ask me for the logic here because normally hats, unless they were associated with a uniform, didn't do it for me. This one had some sort of unit patch or symbol on it but was mostly a dark greenygray color. He had this rugged, manly look that made me want to—

"It's the only rental."

I moved past him, hoping he'd think the color in my cheeks had come from being surprised and not from appreciating the view. "Why would you automatically think the rental was mine?"

He smirked. "You drove yourself on the compound, right?"

"I did."

"So you went past the barbed-wire fence and the big barriers? And then you gave your name to Sam or Geoff?" He folded his arms and leaned back a bit, demonstrating his total comfort.

I pulled open the driver's-side door and chucked my purse onto the passenger seat. "Sure did. Not entirely unlike getting on the main post."

The unit compound was about five miles from the main Fort Liberty land. It had the advantage of being away from all the traffic but from the outside looked more like a highly protected forest area with manufacturing buildings on it. I hadn't gotten a tour of the grounds and hoped I would at some point, but I definitely saw why everyone who worked there lived in the towns out here and not on the main post.

"You may not have noticed that you were escorted. Or that your car information was documented. Or that if you hadn't been on the list, things would've gotten interesting."

I swallowed, feeling a little ignorant and a lot fluttery when he stood and came to face me, my car door between us.

"Okay, fine. Not a lot of tourists toodling around. The bigger question is, what do you want?"

I didn't mean to sound snippy or rude, but he sent my

logic on vacation with his hat and his stupid handsome face and my knowledge of his secretly glorious brain inside of a magnificent body.

And the whole "I just tracked you down in an alley to say goodbye" thing a few weeks ago…

Ugh.

He folded his arms and widened his stance. "I came to ask you out."

Wait. What?

And my brain didn't get any farther than that, so I said, "*What?*"

He smiled, and *hoo, boy,* danger.

"I've been waiting until you came out of the building to ask you out. We're both professionals, so I wanted to make sure it was after work, out of the office. Let's ignore for a moment that we're still technically at work." He gestured to the ground.

I nodded, not sure what else to do. My heart hammered in my chest, and I wanted to burst out laughing. Like, in what world was this happening? But then I also wanted to say *yes, yes, a thousand times yes* because duh. See previous statements about the smarts and the looks and the hat.

Did I want to go out with this man? Yes. And no. Because this timing was all wrong, wasn't it? Every single time we'd seen each other had been wrong. First, I was his test administrator and couldn't cross a professional boundary. Then we were in Budapest and he was literally undercover. And now?

Now I needed to focus on figuring myself out and getting settled. I'd taken a turn getting this job, and I was grateful and excited about the possibilities, but I'd hardly had time to get my bearings. And one thing was very clear when it came to Ryan West—he turned my bearings upside down. Not to mention, the man was a soldier of all soldiers, and if I'd avoided dating soldiers this long, why would I want to start now?

In all honesty, I could admit that was the real issue. The timing could work if I wanted it to, but the reality of his life as not only a soldier but as a part of the EMU?

"So? Emily Wender, can I take you out?"

CHAPTER ELEVEN

West

A little over twenty-four hours after asking her out, Emily Wender slid into the dark polished wood booth across from me.

"Sorry I'm a minute late. It's been another super weird day." She plunked down her purse and grabbed a menu.

I stifled a laugh. Yesterday, I'd effectively surprised her when she walked up and found me sitting on the hood of her car and even more so when I asked her out. Her lashes had fluttered, and she'd bitten her lower lip but hadn't hesitated to agree. She'd simply said, "I'm free tomorrow around four for a drink. Let me know where to meet you."

Had to admit, I liked that. Everything I'd seen and heard about her, I liked, but this ability to stay quick on her toes appealed to me on a core level. I'd given up casually dating years ago when it became an exhausting series of women wanting to date a soldier, only to hold a grudge when the reality of dating one came calling.

Missed dates due to training schedule changes. Canceled plans due to national emergencies my team responded to—of course they never knew that part. But still. I liked that despite the fact I could tell I affected Emily, she kept her cool.

That said, I wouldn't mind heating her up.

For now, I'd focus on the pleasure of her company, the here and now, and we'd take it from there. Admittedly, something in me had shifted from feeling a little panicked, and yet excited to find out she was here when Jimmy first told me, to a sense of calm.

Almost a sense of rightness.

It wasn't once in a blue moon with her—it'd now been three times. If I believed in fate, I'd have the uncanny sense that this, with Emily, was it.

I wasn't a man who'd been wandering around feeling empty and sad because I didn't have a partner. It probably helped that of my small team, South and East hadn't dated in years, and North only occasionally went out with people casually. None of us was paired off, and that made it easy to get together whenever we wanted. Add the fact we trained and traveled quite a bit, and my life was full. I only had so many more years before I'd be edged out of team work and into admin, then into retirement. Plenty of good men I'd worked with had done so recently, and some of them had found a great deal of happiness in retirement. I'd been assuming I'd do the same.

I could also acknowledge that since I'd met Emily, I'd been mulling over possibilities. Not plans, but just... what would it be like to have someone I clicked with like that in the beginning and who I grew to not only care for but love. How would it happen? What would it look like?

And yesterday, some part of me said *let's stick around and find out.*

So here we were.

"What made it a super weird day?" I asked, then nodded at the waitress in thanks as she set down two ice waters.

"Thank you," she said to the woman, then shook her head as her eyes slipped around the room, moving too fast to be taking in details of the place. "I went house hunting, but that wasn't all that exciting. I guess it's just the culture shock of coming back, and then I saw this man I swear I used to see at one of the bodegas near my apartment in Budapest. Probably not—I'm sure my mind is playing tricks on me, but it just added to the surreality of things lately."

Every sense I had narrowed onto that, and my mind ran through possibilities. Could be a coworker who happened to move—unlikely, but we liked to say it was a "small Army" and that went for government work, too. Could be something totally innocent or just a mistake. But it could also be a very, *very* bad sign.

"Was he an American? Or a Hungarian national?"

Her eyes finally met mine. She took a long drink from her water and pressed her lips together like she needed to catch her bearings. "Uh, honestly, I'm not sure. He looked really nondescript, but the way he stood was distinct. I'm not sure I ever realized I noticed him in the city until I just *thought* I saw him today, but I'm sure it's a different guy."

Not necessarily unusual to think you've seen a familiar face, but possibly suspicious. Though perhaps the question lay more with whether she tended to be observant or not. "Is it normal for you to notice men?"

Her eyes slid to the side and her brow furrowed. Her face was so expressive, I could read the "Are you kidding me with this question?" all over it.

"I'm not sure how to answer this question. I do sometimes notice men, when they are... notable."

Maybe South's ghost took over my body—it was the only reason I could possibly have to say, "Like me?"

Her mouth dropped open in a gorgeous display of teeth and humor. "Are you kidding me right now?"

I laughed, glad she didn't just get up and leave. "Yes. I was channeling my buddy South. He's a terrible flirt and I think he must be rubbing off on me more than I realized."

She shook her head but didn't stop grinning. "Is that what you were doing? Flirting with me?"

With a grin and no small amount of delight that she'd take the chance to rib me, I looked up at the waitress as she approached and took our drink orders, plus I suggested a few appetizers and Emily readily agreed. When we were alone again, she fiddled with a cardboard coaster while she spoke.

"To answer your question, yes, you're notable. But not so much physically..."

I shifted. "I'll choose not to be offended by that."

She chuckled. "You shouldn't be. For me, it was the tests." Her eyes flicked up to mine and searched.

I knew the question without her having to ask it. "I grew up speaking French with my mom, who was a native speaker. I studied Spanish in an immersion program from a young age. I went to language school for Arabic and had specific tutoring and work in Pashto. High aptitude, high exposure, lots of training, personal interest, lots of practical use. Nothing fancy."

She exhaled roughly, like my explanation did something

to her, then grinned. "I told my friend Bec about you. She said she didn't believe you actually existed."

"Turns out, I wasn't a figment of your imagination, after all," I said, leaning back against the soft cushion of the booth, anxious to circle back around to this person she'd seen and yet very happy she wasn't afraid to admit she was interested in me.

"So it seems." She tucked her dark shoulder-length hair behind one ear.

I didn't know this woman, didn't have the right to touch her, but the need to feel her hair slide across my skin hit me like a jab to the throat.

I cleared away the sensation and watched the waitress set our drinks and appetizers down before continuing the conversation.

"So you don't normally notice men, but you noticed me."

She rolled her eyes, but I pressed on, not wanting to put too fine a point on my joke and not wanting to worry her.

"And this guy isn't particularly notable, but you saw him today? Do you remember what he looked like?"

She frowned. "Of course. Five foot nine or ten, wiry frame but probably muscular, jeans and a long-sleeved dark gray shirt. Short beard, unremarkable medium-length brown hair."

"So the issue is not that you're unobservant."

She laughed and took a sip of her beer. "Yeah, no. Definitely not the issue. I really thought he was the same person, but he never met my eye, and I haven't been sleeping all that well, so it's probably just me."

I lowered my voice, knowing no one in this place was a suspect, but also leaning into caution. "Where are you staying?"

Not following my logic, her brow furrowed in confusion. "Why does that matter?"

"Hotel? Motel? With a friend?" I prompted, fully used to getting the information I wanted when I asked for it and forgetting to curb the tone I used to get it.

Her expression shifted to something wary, but she said, "A hotel. Not far from here, actually. It's a decent chain place."

"Good. I'll follow you there whenever you want to leave —not to go inside, just to take a look. And you keep watching, too."

Her whole energy changed. "Wait, why? Is he someone dangerous? Do you know who he is?"

"I've been doing what I do long enough to know that coincidences and oddities like what you mentioned can happen. Sometimes, it really is nothing, but sometimes... it's something."

She blinked, worry coloring her features.

Shoot. I didn't mean to scare her. I reached out and set a hand on hers where it rested on the table. "It's probably nothing. But stay aware for me, yeah?"

And in the meantime, I'd get East on it, maybe even some of the nerds—their preferred moniker, never a name I'd choose to give them—at the compound. Maybe they can track Hungarian nationals, make sure no one on our watch list has moved. It could be nothing, but again, everything with Volkov had felt too easy almost. Got the women, caught the mole, burned the cache... maybe this was the other shoe dropping.

"Um, yeah, okay. But—"

"Well, what do we have here? Is Big Daddy West on a date at our team bar?"

CHAPTER TWELVE

Emily

A giant of a man dragged a chair to the end of our booth and sat down on it backward. His cheesy grin swung from me to West like he'd never had a better moment in his life than this one, then he popped a lollypop into the corner of his mouth like a grade schooler.

A familiar man jogged up with his thick Clark Kent glasses, wavy dark hair, and a ten o'clock shadow, and pulled the big one up by the back of his shirt, biceps flexing with the effort. "I told this idiot not to bug you guys. Sorry, Emily."

I glanced at West to see him mildly amused by these two while I smiled at North in recognition.

"This bozo is Scott Wexler, who we affectionately call South, and his less irritating friend there, who you may remember, is North *Kaplan*, also known as North."

"Nice to see you again," North said with a smile.

"South, this is Emily Wender." West tipped his head toward me.

South extended a hand. "Nice to meet you, Emily. We were wondering why this guy couldn't meet us earlier, and now we see why."

North elbowed him in the ribs. "What brings you to North Carolina, and how'd you end up here with this fella?"

Okay, so North was absolutely adorable, which I'd noticed before, but it glared at me now, even through his lightly couched interrogation that failed to sound casual enough. South looked like he could crush a man with one hand, but he also had a very friendly smile with a few crooked bottom teeth that made him a little more human. And that lollypop... Both men, like the one who sat across from me, were stupidly handsome. Honestly, where was the EMU finding these guys?

"We ran into each other yesterday, actually." *At your place of work.* But I wouldn't say that, just in case it brushed up against the non-disclosure agreement I'd signed.

"Remind me where you met in the first place?" North asked, squinting.

"Kugelfels, Germany." Something about the way he asked made me certain he already knew the answer, which eased on the interrogation vibe. It felt like catching up. Awkward, but slightly more comfortable nevertheless.

"Were you working at the ed center? You ran this guy's DLPTs?" North tipped his head to the side.

My stomach flipped as West blushed. Before I could answer or fully appreciate the sight, South let out an, "Ohhh! Way to throw his game, man!" and laughed into his hand.

North's eyes got big, but then he blinked and a mask fell

into place. "What? I recall him commenting on what a well-run testing center it was."

I grinned but held in a laugh. West just didn't bother—he laughed lightly and smiled back.

And goodness, I liked this so much. This willingness not to get angry or weird about the fact that his friend had just let it slip he'd told them about me. Maybe it really was just about my testing center and how well I'd administered his tests, but based on the faint blush? It'd been more than that.

"Well, East'll be here soon." South addressed me. "Our fourth team member, Shane Easton. You'll know he's here when the mood darkens and a sense of brooding silence not unlike a black hole steps through the door." North and West chuckled quietly before South added, "You guys joining us for a drink in a bit?"

The giant man stood and stepped back from his seat, then picked up the solid wood chair with a finger hooked around the top piece of wood.

I eyed West, realizing he'd brought me to the place where he already had plans. I didn't know what to think of it, or what to say.

"I'll let you know. See you guys," West said, not taking his eyes from me. As soon as they stepped away, he leaned forward. "I wanted you to meet them, but they weren't supposed to be here until five. Obviously, you met North and I wondered if maybe you'd seen South and East last week, and I figured it might be nice to know some other people at work. I'm also fairly unoriginal when it comes to where to get a drink, since this is the only place I ever go."

I took a sip of my beer and processed that. It fit him that he had a solid routine and liked what he liked, plus I felt a wedge of something like honored that he'd bring me to the same place he spent time with his team. At the same time, I wondered...

"This is where you bring all your dates?"

One of his brows lifted, but he didn't respond. I didn't know whether that meant yes, or no, or *what other dates?* But look at the man—there had to be other dates.

Unless there weren't *dates* so much as... *rendezvouses.*

"I don't know what that look is, but go ahead and tell me. Let's get whatever your concerns are out in the open." He sat back, thumb and index finger resting against the bottom of his pint glass.

"That's not a very first date-type question, is it?" I tipped my head to the side, trying to take in all of him. There was a lot to enjoy and it was all very nice.

Plenty of height and hair styled longer on top than the sides but neatly kempt. His trimmed beard had flashes of gold and auburn in the dark hairs, and his blue eyes were somehow even bluer than usual, though maybe that impression was due to finally looking at him closely without pretending I wasn't.

I even liked his hands—the way they looked a little rough paired with the memory of fleeting handshakes and touches and the possessive, warm grip on my waist weeks ago.

Maybe best of all, he seemed completely himself. No false modesty or games afoot here, if I had to guess. Ironic, considering what I now knew he did for a living, but I'd bet money this was just Ryan West, no covers or masks, sitting across from me after all this time.

"Is this a first date?" He angled his head to match mine.

I straightened, knocked off-balance by the question. "You did ask me out."

"Yes, but I don't normally take women out on dates to bars for a drink at four in the afternoon."

"No?"

"Nope. I'd normally do dinner. I'd normally pick her up. Granted, *normally* implies I do this all the time, and I don't, so you can get that concern off your list. I'm not dating anyone else, Emily, and I don't want to."

I shifted in my seat. *Direct, much?* I hadn't dated at all in Budapest, but anytime I went out in Germany, it was a lot of vague answers and "let's live in the moment" language. This man was quite the opposite of that, and I told him so. "Uh, okay. That's kind of a lot."

A hint of a smile tugged at his mouth. "I'm kind of a lot."

I chuckled, a bit of tension loosening. "Yeah. I'm getting that."

"Good."

"Is this your way of warning me off? Should I be planning my exit?" Part joke, part genuine question.

Despite his mildly pushy way of talking now, and the intensity of his whole... being... I liked him. I'd been thinking about him for actual years and wasn't about to get scared away by a little flair of alpha male. I was an alpha female when I wanted to be—I got it. The question was, would he? Or was he expecting me to be someone he could boss around?

He leaned his forearms on the table again, then ducked his head and spoke quietly. It gave me a sense of tunnel vision, like there was no one else in the ever-busier pub than the two of us.

"I'd rather you not leave, but I do want you to understand right now. I don't have time for games and I'm not a casual kind of guy. So if that's what you want, or if you need more time to get settled before you dive into something, or if you have anyone else waiting in the wings you've been thinking about, go ahead and say the word."

I swallowed. Maybe the beer hit my mostly empty stomach or more likely it was the fault of those blue eyes boring into me. It was a man lethal enough to be in the Exceptional Mission Unit speaking to me like he'd thought about me, too, since we'd first met. Not just while we overlapped in Budapest and not just since then. For a while now.

Whatever it was, I didn't hesitate to respond. My gut might be lit by fireflies right now, I might have major reservations about starting something with anyone, let alone a super soldier, but I also had an eerie sense that this was already written.

I'd had it before—the day Bec came into my office years ago in Fort Campbell. The day I got the offer to move to Kugelfels.

The day Ryan West entered the ed center and ever so politely begged me to let him take back-to-back tests all week on the promise he'd pass them all.

And so, despite the knowledge that he was exactly the kind of man I shouldn't want to date considering his job and what that meant for his life, I spoke honestly. "There's no one else I'm interested in."

He nodded.

"And I appreciate no games. I can also appreciate not wanting casual, too, but since I don't know you, I can't speak to that yet. I can say I'm open to something, and that so far even this whole thing you've got going on"—I gestured to his general presence—"isn't making me hesitate."

He smiled. My heart did a little tuck jump.

"But I just want to be clear about something."

"Okay."

"I'm new in town. New at my job. I'm off-kilter here, and I don't know you. So we're casual until we know each other."

He shook his head. "No."

My eyes widened, somehow shocked by the answer, though having heard it, I should've known it was coming. "Pardon?"

"I have no interest in dating you casually. If you're interested, be interested in *me*. Date me, get to know me, and let's see how we mesh. But it won't be casual."

"Heyyy!"

South's voice raising in greeting to a third man who clearly belonged with this crew caught my attention and I glanced over. West's eyes were still wholly focused on me when I looked back at him.

"I wonder if maybe we have different definitions of casual. I guess what I mean is, I'm not committed to anything with you until I decide I am. It concerns me you're saying—"

He covered my hand with his large, warm, rough one. My skin ignited under his touch, and I had to force myself to focus on his words.

"I'm not trying to be a jerk. I've just been burned before."

I blinked again at that. Wow. I had *not* expected that. "You have?"

"Yeah. Women who wanted to date me and a handful of other dudes at the same time. They wanted to *keep it casual*. And good for them, but that's not right for me. I want a future with someone, so I'm not wasting my time with people who aren't also looking for something serious—even if that might not end up working between us. You're not obligated to me, obviously, but if you want to see me again, I'd prefer you *only* see me."

Was this weird? I needed to call Bec or Katie and see because it kind of was, but at the same time, who the heck else was I about to date? And realistically, I'd never dated more than one person at a time. I found someone, dated him, it fizzled out, I moved on. I just didn't recall anyone bringing this up on a non-first-date, but something told me West was unconventional in more ways than one.

Actually, it was kind of European of him. Despite what Americans might believe, I'd witnessed a great deal of monogamy and serious relationships among people my age and younger there, and a lot less casual dating. *Huh.*

Also, sorry, but who else would you date if you're dating the physical manifestation of Captain America and he's like, kind of *actually* Captain America minus the whole sleeping since WWII and waking up to join the Avengers deal? Where do you go from that?

Maybe these past women had held the same reservations I did—the concern over what life with him would really be like when he was constantly flying off and doing dangerous work, leaving behind everything but his team.

Though, even now, my worry over what that would look like for *me* with him felt somehow... thin.

To make sure I didn't seem put off by the idea of focusing on him, I spoke up. "That's fine—I won't be dating anyone else while I get to know you. I assume it goes both ways?"

He gave me a half smile and squeezed my hand before pulling his back to his side of the booth. *Sad.*

"It definitely goes both ways."

CHAPTER THIRTEEN

Later, after my time alone with her—we'd been talking for half an hour—we joined the guys, and Emily hadn't faltered for a second. Not when South gave her crap or when she asked about their nicknames and they acted like she'd mortally offended them. Even East got in on it, though that was just him staying silent, which meant he could be *in* or *out* of anything depending on the perspective.

When he looked directly at her and didn't speak but only tipped his chin down slightly in response to her greeting, she smiled wide. "I see you're the chatty one."

She won a half smile from the man, which only made her beam. When South offered her a high five, she met his palm with a loud smack.

"Ketchup, woman. You give good five."

She cackled. "Uh, mustard, and thank you?"

He grinned. "Nah, I just mean, I approve. You're not scared of East's glower or my awesomeness. I assume North's nerdy good looks haven't upset you, either, and so I'm saying you're good people."

I rolled my eyes and prepared to tell South off for insinuating his approval had anything to do with things, but she just chuckled and said, "So are you."

She didn't miss a beat all evening, and even though I'd seen her glance at me a few times, she hadn't leaned on me. She hadn't *needed* me to navigate the discussion with my best friends.

That was exactly why I was serious about her—she stood on her own two feet in every sense. It was one of several reasons I'd wanted to cut through the usual crap of a first date and put it out there. I hated casual. I didn't want it with her. So if we kept at this, I needed to know she might want something more.

All signs pointed to yes, even if I had definitely taken her off guard by being so upfront about my desires. A few days ago, I might've taken myself off guard, but I was a man who didn't waver. I didn't have to argue with myself on this —things were settling down at work. Yes, missions would pop up when some wannabe terrorist faction hijacked a plane or kidnapped some missionaries, but we'd solve that problem when it came. Volkov was going down between what we'd just accomplished and what the other teams out there were working on, and it was all going to change things in Europe and have global ripples.

She'd get used to that quickly. I didn't have time or interest in playing games, didn't want to keep her on the hook if she wanted off, and certainly didn't want to waste the time I had with someone who didn't plan on marrying or having kids ultimately.

We hadn't gone *there* just yet, but we'd get there. Maybe we'd get all the way there.

Every brush of fingertips sent my pulse racing. When she bent over laughing at some idiot non-expletive South used, I couldn't keep the wild grin from my cheeks. She wasn't afraid to have fun and be joyful, and she made everything bright.

Already.

Carefree. Unreserved. Certainly no pretense or airs about her.

What would that be like? To have that all the time? To come home to her and laugh with her and have these moments with my friends and my—well, with Emily?

I'd never had this reaction to anyone. I'd felt it years ago in Germany, and despite my best efforts not to think about her after the mission, it'd been unavoidable. And I could lean on her should I need to. She'd kept my secret, she'd trusted that I wasn't there doing something bad— maybe we needed to talk about that, actually. But not just yet.

"Where'd you look? You gotta have your real estate agent check out our neighborhood." South pulled out his phone, and if I had to guess, was pulling up an aerial view of our neighborhood.

"Oh, uh, I can't live on post as a single GS—"

"Nah, we're out here in the pines. We're in Sunny Pines. It's this little tiny area right next to Aberdeen and Southern Pines. You'd miss it if you didn't know it was there, which is how we like it." He handed Emily the phone.

She studied it. "That is pretty small." Her eyes flicked up to mine. "Is it all... soldiers?"

North answered first. "No, there are a few military

unaffiliated people. Then there's GS and contractors. And of course, there's Southy's girlfriend."

South shot daggers at North before swinging his head to Emily. "She's a friend. She's got cute kids. She's not military—not anymore. And this doofus calls her my girlfriend because I'm nice to her and I help her out sometimes. She lives right next to me—am I not supposed to be friendly?"

Emily patted his arm. "I'm sure you're a great neighbor. She's lucky to live by you."

North made a gesture I was glad Emily missed. East's eyes held a smile even if the rest of him was stone-faced.

"Are there any houses for sale?" she asked, handing the phone back to South, then caught my eye. "I wouldn't want to encroach on your little EMU hideaway. Oops, that slipped. I'm sorry."

I nudged her elbow with mine, though what I really wanted to do was sling an arm around her shoulders and press a kiss to her temple. This sudden rush of affection and the desire to protect her would probably get me slapped if I let it drive, so I parked it.

"You're a part of EMU now, too, so you qualify." I winked to let her know I didn't give a damn about what people did for work. They needed to be decent humans, good neighbors, and they'd be welcomed.

"Well, maybe I'll see if I can drive through tomorrow and check some things out."

"Hey, you should just come to the barbecue at West's. It's at four tomorrow. There'll be a ton of people there from work, and then you can see the area."

North said this so cheerily, it was clear he didn't realize how weird it was for him to be asking her to come to the barbecue.

South heard it, though. "Good grief. Nerd alert North,

did you hear yourself? You just invited West's woman to a barbecue at West's house."

Emily bit her lip, clearly feeling a little awkward. I didn't like the idea that anything would make her uncomfortable, let alone feel uninvited. As far as I was concerned, she had a standing invitation to anything I did that she could be privy to, but saying as much would probably be an overload.

"I had planned to invite you, if it seemed like you wanted to get together again. So, yes, please come tomorrow, if you want."

Her eyes flickered between mine like she might be able to tell if I was just placating her or covering up for North's misstep. She could look all she wanted—she wouldn't see anything but just that. I wanted to see her again, and if I could do so tomorrow, all the better.

"Okay. I'll let you know tomorrow, if that's okay."

Shoot, I liked this woman. How long had it been since I'd been with someone who didn't automatically do what I wanted? And she wasn't even putting me off just to show she could—she very well might have plans. She had connections everywhere, from what I'd already seen and heard, and she may not actually have time to spend another afternoon with me. But hopefully, she'd want to.

"Sounds good."

She checked her watch. "I should probably go."

"I'll head, too."

"Oh, you gonna escort her home?" South batted his eyelashes like an absolute idiot before grabbing a handful of pub fries and disappearing them into his giant mouth.

I gave him a hard look. "As a matter of fact, I am. And for good reason. She saw someone she thought she'd seen in Budapest."

All three of the men straightened in their seats while Emily hopped down, seemingly oblivious to the change in mood with her back turned as she gathered her purse. Each man nodded at me, silently getting the message that we'd be discussing this soon and definitely understanding why I'd be driving behind her and making sure she got to her hotel.

After farewells and the short drive to her hotel, I got a text from East right as I parked. *"Our friend in the E may have a man on the ground. More research needed. Stay frosty."*

Not good news if Volkov had someone here. East must've called into work to check after I left—had to thank him for that. He had no tolerance for waiting on information—another irony since he was one of the most patient people I'd ever met.

But this meant whoever Emily had seen earlier was most likely with Volkov directly or somehow connected. It made no sense for them to interact with her unless they thought she could do something for them, which meant they'd be approaching her soon if they really had someone here. All around not good news, because it wouldn't be something we could nail down overnight.

I hopped out of the car and came up with a hand on her back. "We're walking in together, okay?"

She looked up at me, definitely bewildered by my sudden closeness. "Uh, okay."

I slid my hand down to wrap around her hip and spoke into her ear. "Talk to me like you like me. Like you're mine."

She huffed out a breath but didn't miss a beat when she leaned up and her lips grazed my ear. "I don't know what I'd do any differently if I was—I'd still be confused about what the heck is going on."

Doing my best to ignore the ripples of sensation

coasting along the shell of my ear and down my neck and resisting a smile because even in moments of stress she could be so damn clever, I straightened and surveyed every bit of the parking lot, forested area nearby, lobby, hallway—nothing suspicious. I hadn't expected someone to follow her, especially since they'd approached her earlier. They'd already been following her. They undoubtedly knew where she was staying if they'd found her at the grocery store.

When we reached her room, I closed a hand over hers that held the key and pulled it out, then opened the door and shut it behind us, barging in front of her to check the bathroom.

"Um, hi, please come into my hotel room despite our knowing each other for approximately five seconds." Her tone conveyed her annoyance.

I came to stand in front of her. "I'm sorry to get pushy on you, but there's a good chance you've been watched or followed or both. I don't know why, but I'm going to figure it out."

Alarm shot through her with a physical jolt and her eyes widened. "Why? What makes you think that?"

"The guy you saw today... I'm not saying it's certain, but it doesn't sit right."

She turned to look around the room like the answer to whatever was going on might be hidden in a corner. "What do I do about that? How do I get them to stop?"

Something about the question cut through the adrenaline and the list I'd compiled in my head of next steps. I set my hands on her shoulders. "You're going to be okay. You're going to sleep here tonight, do your thing tomorrow, and stay aware. Anyone approaches you, you bug out. Anyone follows you in your car, pull into the police station, or come to the compound. You know about Jordan?"

She shook her head. "Jordan?"

"If you're under duress, someone's in the car with you or behind you, whatever, you tell the gate guard your friend Jordan's coming to visit and they'll know something's up."

If possible, her eyes widened further, but she gripped my wrists. "Wait, seriously? This is serious? I don't, uh—" She cleared her throat. "I don't know what to do."

"You're going to be fine. Do what I said—stay aware. Stick to the plans you already had. And come to the barbecue tomorrow. We've got plenty of surveillance in the neighborhood, so we'll know if someone's tailing you. It'll be a perfect way to flush 'em out. And until then, I'll see what I can do."

My phone had buzzed no fewer than six times since I'd entered her room. I hated to leave her, but I couldn't stay. That wouldn't be wise for a few reasons, but mostly because I needed to figure out what their next move was and stop it before they so much as laid eyes on Emily again. The hotel had twenty-four-hour staffing and if the person was here and didn't make contact earlier, there was less of a chance they'd do so now.

And sure... maybe it was all a coincidence.

"I've got to go. I'll see you tomorrow, though, and you have my number?" I stepped toward the door.

Her wide eyes followed me. "Um, yeah. Yes. Okay. I can do that. I—I can do that."

I turned back, unable to stop myself from pulling her into a hug. She gripped me around my waist, her hands pressing into my back. I kissed her temple, relieved for this second of closeness even if it didn't make sense.

"I'll see you tomorrow."

CHAPTER FOURTEEN

Emily

I made it through the night. We'll say it that way since even pretending I slept or did anything more than existed and didn't leave my room would be a gross exaggeration.

It's funny how even as an adult, it feels safer under the covers. I sat there huddled under the hotel comforter with my book until the sun rose this morning. Any time I got up, I felt more vulnerable.

West would laugh at that. What a silly notion—that somehow, my blanky would keep me safe. There'd be no protection from anyone who came into this room, blanket or no. And the fact I even needed to think about it made me mildly ill, though it could absolutely be the fear-induced insomnia talking.

Here's the thing. I wasn't a hysterical person. I didn't react emotionally a lot because that wasn't my default. Did I have human emotions? Heck yes. Did I cry and rage and find myself overwhelmed? I did indeed. But I was also solidly in my mid-thirties, had lived alone since I was eighteen, and didn't scare easily.

But when a man like West tells me to stay put, to stay alert, that isn't something I can just yoga flow my way through.

I messaged Noah and Katie and said something weird was going on. They asked me to come stay with them, but I worried about bringing whatever this mess was to their door. They had a toddler and Katie was pregnant. Noah was a great soldier, but what could he do in the middle of the night? He would protect his wife and child with his life, and I respected that completely—enough so I wouldn't dare bring any of this around them.

West hadn't said I was unsafe here, but the longer the night wore on, the more frustrated I felt. Who tells a woman she's maybe in danger but then basically says, "Just stay inside." What kind of answer to the problem was that?

Oh, I had tried to brush it off. I had attempted to distract myself, to sink into the latest Josie Wade romance I had on my ereader and live happily ever ignorant, but my mind ran away. I kept thinking about the man I'd seen, begging my brain to highlight the details that were similar to the man from Budapest. And then, what was different? *Was it the same person?*

I waffled back and forth. It couldn't have been. It made no sense for it to be. But West had taken me seriously... a weirdly encouraging thing, but also a terrible one. Because if he really believed something was wrong, then maybe it was. He'd seen a lot more of the world, and a lot more of whatever bad guys Budapest held.

So eventually, just after midnight, I called him. Yep, just

called, not even a text, so that illustrated how far gone my reason was at the time.

"Em. You okay?"

His urgency fueled my own, brushing past the embarrassment of my call. "Nothing happened. I just... I'm scared. This is so stupid. I'm probably wrong, right?"

"It's not stupid to be scared. And yes, it could be nothing. But don't shame yourself for being scared. That can keep you alert."

His voice was calming and measured, which I absolutely needed right now.

"I'm just not used to this," I admitted.

"To feeling scared?"

Would he think of me as weak if I owned up to it? Would he scoff at how helpless I was, how pathetically I was handling even a small *possible* threat when he spent his days rescuing hostages and hunting down terrorists?

But there was no point in denying it, either, was there? All my independence and choices in the last fifteen-plus years of my life didn't mean squat when it came to actual danger. I couldn't protect myself. I couldn't work my way out of this or solve the problem through grit and determination and the refusal to lean on someone else. I *needed* someone else, and it was painful.

But I didn't swallow the truth like my instincts begged me to. For once, I let someone else see. "Yes."

A beat passed, and then he said, "It's okay to be scared. You're a smart woman and you're not alone."

I laughed. "I am literally alone right now."

He chuckled. "In this. You're not alone in all of this. We'll figure it out."

I swallowed hard, feeling reassured and yet still wishing

I could forget all about the man I'd thought I'd seen. "Okay, thank you."

"What's something you love? Something in your daily routine you look forward to?" His voice came steady and quiet, as though we were having a regular conversation and this wasn't a call rooted in fear.

"Uh, why are you asking that?"

He chuckled. "Humor me, okay?"

Guess I could. I had called him, after all. "Uh, tea? I love tea."

"You like it with a little milk, no sugar, right?"

I startled, sitting up in the bed. "Yes. It's a good ritual—the routine of steeping, adding milk, the first sip being a touch too hot and then drinking it slowly as I arrange my brain for the day. But how could you know that?"

"I'm an observant man."

I sighed dramatically. "Will you ever share your secrets, or is this how it's going to be?"

A beat of quiet passed before he spoke again. "I'll tell you whatever you want to know. Just ask. If I can tell you, I will."

The sincerity in his voice and his words shocked me into a moment of silence, but soon enough, I rallied and said, "Well, what's something you love?"

"I'm more of a coffee drinker myself, but I've had enough days where there's no coffee up for grabs, so I wouldn't say that. I think my favorite part of a day is dawn."

In my mind's eye, I could see the scruff of his beard and the blue of his eyes. I wondered if he was on the couch or in bed, relaxing or still pulsing with that readiness he exuded whenever I saw him. I wouldn't have guessed his answer in a million years.

"Dawn?"

He hummed in confirmation. "It's not something I see every day, of course, but I love it. It's... hopeful."

I closed my eyes, savoring this small insight. "That's lovely."

A breathy chuckle came before he said, "Guess it is, kind of. But also true."

"What do you love about your job?" I asked, hoping he'd share a little more of himself in the spirit of distracting me, which he was clearly doing and I appreciated so much.

"Mm, I'd probably give you different answers at different times in my career. But now?" He was quiet for a moment before he continued. "It may sound cliché, but I like making a difference. I like knowing I'm stopping someone bad or saving someone from something bad. And no, it's not simply *bad* and *good*, but there are objectively evil things in the world and sometimes, I get to be part of the team that stops it. That makes it worth it."

My heart squeezed. "Like saving Janie and Nancy?"

"If that were something I'd done, then yes. Like that."

I laughed softly and exhaled a sense of satisfaction or maybe even peace. It was a simple conversation, but an honest one, and it felt wondrously valuable. It allowed me to see the man behind the persona. It made me see Ryan.

"Thank you for answering when I called."

"Always. If you need me, I can be there in ten minutes. Do you want me to come?"

His words hung between us, and I wanted to reach out and claim them. I wanted to say yes. He wouldn't have offered if he didn't mean it. But I also hated the thought of him having to drive this late, to come coddle me because I couldn't handle the possibility of something. And I did feel less anxious after getting out of my head a bit.

Part of me had expected him to insist on staying with

me all night. When I called, part of me had hoped he'd be here in a minute and I'd hear a knock on my door because he'd been expecting to hear from me. But as pushy as he could be, he wasn't going to plow over what I wanted or mow down my independence, and I had to appreciate this. Especially now that we'd shared this small conversation in the dark of night and he'd been here for me in another way, if not standing in the room with me.

I felt so out of my league it hurt—I couldn't take care of myself, and I didn't know how to be as open as he was, as sure as he was. But I did know what he'd already done to distract and calm me, and I didn't want to press for more, so I summoned my answer. "No. I'll be okay. I'll see you tomorrow."

"If you change your mind, I'm a call away."

We hung up after that, and I did my best impression of a sleeping person until the sun rose. Instead of only thinking of the man I thought I'd seen, I circled around West's answers and the feeling in the pit of my stomach that I'd love to witness him at dawn, just to see him see it. Just to watch this warrior of a man in the soft morning glow of the distant rising sun and see what hope looked like on his handsome face.

Ultimately, I rolled out of bed feeling relieved for morning and more than ready for daylight.

By two in the afternoon, I couldn't stand to be in the hotel another minute. I'd ordered in food, done every bit of online house hunting and correspondence I could think of, watched an hour of anxiety-inducing news, and finally got dressed and left the room in a kind of rage- and exhaustion-fueled whirlwind in which I convinced myself that if anyone approached me, I'd knee them in the family jewels and run now and ask questions later.

I'd mapped the nearest police and fire stations in case I noticed anyone following me but then admitted to myself I likely wouldn't know if someone was following me unless they were terrible at it. Since I hadn't noticed anyone yet, I suspected I wouldn't ever.

I drove to Sunny Pines. I'd decided I'd burn an hour driving around the neighborhood before showing up at West's because I was not about to be early and seem even more needy than my midnight phone call had made me, and in the meantime, I could scope out any homes for sale. I also took solace in the thought that there was at least a small handful of EMU operators and military personnel just about everywhere in the area, so if something weird happened, I could try to scream really loudly and maybe they'd come running.

Yeah, I rolled my eyes at myself. But I had to keep it light in my head and imagine whoever was following me as a caricature of a bad guy instead of someone scary and actually nefarious.

I'd stopped outside a home with a for sale sign in the yard and was pulling up the listing online to see about pricing and interior details when someone knocked on my window and scared my skeleton out of my body. Yep, just like that, the entirety of my bone structure fled in a cartoon poof and I dribbled onto the driver's-side floor mat.

"Emily?"

The man bent down, and sure enough, it was South's giant smile greeting me. I rolled down the window. "Hey."

His grin widened. "You okay?"

I blinked, assessing. I was actually still a corporeal being and not a ghost, so there was a small victory. "You scared me."

"A little jumpy today?"

"Uh, yeah, you think?"

He nodded, which somehow I correctly interpreted as him suggesting I get out of the car. I exited and then fully took him in. Running shoes, ankle socks, tiny army green shorts, no shirt over his broad, ripped chest, and tattoos covering the majority of his pecs, shoulders, and upper arms.

"See something you like?" he asked, fully smirking.

"I'm just appreciating God's creation, is all," I said, fluttering my lashes.

He burst out laughing, face to the sky. "Oh, you'll do nicely."

"What does that mean?"

He made a face but changed the subject when he tipped his head to the side and said, "West is anxious to see you. Let's go inside and he can update you."

"Is it okay for me to leave my car here?" I looked around, confirming I wasn't insane and this wasn't West's block.

"Oh, right. Yeah, you can drive over. I'll meet you there."

"I can give you a ride, if you want."

He waved me away. "Nah, I'm all sweaty. See you in a sec." Then off he went, jogging at a pace that would be a nearly impossible sprint for me.

Two minutes later, I stopped in front of a modest house with a little porch complete with a swing. The landscaping was perfect—healthy green grass, trimmed bushes, blooming flowers.

It wasn't at all a surprise that West's yard looked immaculate, though I wondered how he managed it with being gone so often. Or at least, I imagined it was often, but maybe my impression was wrong, too. Based on the briefings from my new work, the teams were in and out with training and missions, so he must have hired help.

South's knock didn't murder me quite as effectively this time, so I slipped out of the car, grabbing my paltry chips and jarred salsa offering. Someday, I'd wow them with the handful of dishes I could cook—maybe some of my favorites that my amazing food-obsessed friend Summer Masters had taught me. But now? I congratulated myself for not showing up empty-handed.

I started for the door, but South stopped me. "Nah, come around back."

Awkwardness sloshed through me. I'd been on one date with this man, I'd had a crush on him for years, and I'd never been to his house before. Now, I was waltzing in the side gate with his half-naked friend and I felt *weird*.

As a confident person, I didn't love that feeling, but it only spoke to how much I liked this guy and how different all of this was. Had I *ever* shown up to a guy's house for a casual get-together before we'd ever been on a real date? No. It crossed some kind of unspoken boundary of formality, something that said you needed to feel out the other person before getting folded into their social circle.

But West and I weren't normal in any sense of the word, so this made sense, I supposed.

"Chill, Em. We all go this way because he's always back here, especially before a barbecue. You're fine."

I attempted to straighten out my spine and shoulders so I didn't look so obviously uncomfortable, but after the night I'd had, maybe there was no hope for it anyway.

"Hey! Glad you made it, Emily!"

North came toward me, all adorable smile and geeky-chic glasses. Oh, and board shorts and a T-shirt with flip-flops. Totally casual, so at least I'd gotten it right and my white sundress wasn't out of place.

North shook my hand, then put an arm around my shoulders and drew me further into the yard.

And, wow, what a yard it was. An in-ground pool, lush green grass, a little rose garden, and pots brimming with happy, vibrant flowers. There was a pergola tenting over cushy patio chairs and a small sofa with a large fire pit in the middle. Outdoor lights were strung all over. I couldn't wait to see this place when the sun went down.

"You doing okay?" North asked, pulling my attention back to him.

"Oh, yes."

He waited patiently, like he knew there was more to that thought.

"Actually... kind of is a better answer. I didn't sleep last night, and I think I'm going to exhaust my adrenal system from the slightest sound of breeze in the trees."

He pulled me to him in a friendly side hug. "Sorry. We'll get you sorted out. West will give you the update, but we've got a plan in place."

This caused another adrenaline spike to shoot throughout my veins. I needed a plan? Though I guessed that's what these guys did, so I should take it as a good thing, not something to be concerned about.

Mostly, I wanted to see him. Especially after our conversation last night, those small revelations about him that made him feel less like a soldier badass and more like a man. I liked South and North, but West put me at ease in the same breath he knocked me off-kilter in the best way. He'd taken it upon himself to check my room and give me instructions to keep me safe, and as much as I kind of wanted to yell at him for freaking me out, I also appreciated that he didn't just dump me at the front door or tell me I was seeing things. His desire to make things right—to help people, ultimately, wasn't a surprising piece of information as much as it was another piece in the puzzle of West.

And finally, there he was. He slipped out the sliding glass door and onto the patio, a paper-thin T-shirt and shorts showing off an even more fantastically muscular body than I'd seen before, and set a plate of corn on the side of a giant grill.

It was so supremely domestic and familiar. I'd seen him in business casual at the testing center and in a tux, and dressed nicely for our first-ish date, but this was so down to earth and comfortable, and I could practically hear him chide a son or daughter for throwing a ball too close to the grill while he snuck them fruit punch or whatever it was dads who stayed home and grilled for their families did.

Whoa. One late-night conversation and I was picturing Ryan West as a dad. *Really, Emily? We go from staunch independence to fantasizing about babies? Pick a lane!*

"Emily's here, Westy. Come greet your guest," South hollered.

West's head snapped to the side and his eyes found mine in an instant. A familiar, delicious heat spread throughout me, and the ever-heightening anxiety that'd grown monstrous as the time had ticked on since he'd left last night and only halted during our call took a deep breath.

North and South disappeared into the yard or into another universe, and West approached, face serious and eyes intense and so blue they probably made the sky blush. He ducked his head and set his hands on my bare arms. The warmth and feel of his skin on mine sent another wave of heat through me.

"Glad you're here," he said, then leaned forward and pressed a slow, lingering kiss to my cheek.

"Uh—um, me too." *Okay so we have some room to grow on communication with this man.*

He smiled, then grabbed my hand. "Come with me. We have a few things to discuss."

And as though I trusted him implicitly, I followed without question. Because weirdly, *insanely*, I did.

CHAPTER FIFTEEN

West

She followed me without protest, which I took as both a good and bad sign. Good that she seemed to trust me enough to come into my house but bad in that I would've expected a quip of some kind.

"This is really nice," she said as we walked into the living room.

"It's home." Kind of a stupid response, but I didn't want to talk about décor. "Have a seat."

She took a spot on the worn brown leather couch and followed me with laser eyes until I sat across from her in a chair at the edge of the cushion so we weren't too far apart.

"We're looking for intel. We're going to figure this out. But for the time being, do you have any family you could stay with?"

Her eyes shifted away, then back to me. "If I did, I wouldn't want them involved in whatever is going on."

"I can see that. So, no family?" Forgive me if I was digging for more information about the woman herself in the midst of all this.

"My parents retired to Florida not long ago, but we're not particularly close. I have friends locally, but I'm not getting them anywhere near this. So no." She crossed her arms tightly across her chest.

I leaned my elbows on my knees and just leveled with her. "It's possible someone saw you in the elevator with me that night, or more likely, at the café."

Her gaze stayed on me, waiting for more. She wasn't going to flip out. She was solid, even in the midst of something stressful. *Point to Wender*.

"Since we'd spoken earlier with Ambassador Kline, they assumed we were connected. My sitting down with you over coffee likely only confirmed that. Which means they are *still* assuming you know something."

She shifted, crossing her legs.

"Long story short? You might be on their radar. You might not. This could all be a case of mistaken recognition. But I don't like the idea of ignoring your gut." Too many of us had personal experience with how poorly that could go.

She shook her head and exhaled slowly. "This is... it's not too much? Like, you really think there could be someone here who's from whatever bad guy coalition you guys were dealing with in Hungary? Doesn't that seem a little far-fetched?"

The skepticism in her words would've been harsher if it weren't for the way her brows pinched and her whole body broadcasted worry.

I grabbed her hand and pressed it between mine. I wasn't about to explain just how far-reaching the network we thought we'd hamstrung by catching the mole was. It was an international operation and that was just Volkov. We'd hardly begun to make progress toward identifying and taking down the head of the Talon Network.

She wasn't cleared for any specifics anyway, so instead, I kept it simple with something I didn't love admitting but could be true. "It might be. Maybe I'm blowing this way out of proportion."

Her jaw dropped. "I did *not* expect you to say that."

I chuckled low. "No? Well, it might be true. I can't separate what I've done for the last twelve years from my everyday life. I'm great at compartmentalizing things, but I can't ignore coincidences. I should probably work on that. And it's a best-case scenario if I'm totally off on this, right?"

She swallowed hard and nodded.

"Exactly. So, I think the best plan is to be cautious and acknowledge there *could* be something going on, but move ahead as though everything's fine."

She extracted her hand from mine and leaned back, taking a long breath like she needed a minute to digest my suggestion.

"I'm not sure how to do that. I... my mind keeps running away with what-ifs." Then she cleared her throat and abruptly stood. "You know what? No. It'll be fine. You're telling me we'll be cautious and I can do that. Plus, I'll be working... that should be pretty secure, right?"

I laughed at that. "Yeah, pretty secure." Or, one of the most secure facilities in the US. "And listen, without saying too much, we're not done with Budapest. We made progress, major progress, but we're waiting on some more information before we head back to Europe to... follow up."

That was already saying too much, technically, but at least she had basic clearances. And if I had my way, we'd be spending a lot of time together until I left again.

Her face fell. "Oh, so you'll be leaving again?"

My chest pinched. Normally, a woman expressing disappointment at my leaving this early in a relationship wouldn't elicit this kind of reaction. Usually, I'd be a touch annoyed, frankly, because this was the job. But with her, right now, I hated it.

"Could be next week, might be longer. Not sure how long we'll be gone, but you'll be in the groove by then, and again, I think you're good. You only have tomorrow and then you'll be at work. The hotel is reasonably secure. And Rob will be back before I leave, so let's make sure he's tuned in... just in case."

She huffed and rubbed a hand along the smooth skin of her upper arm. "Yeah, I feel like all of that is great, but it also sounds very intense. I'll be traveling for work for a bit, too. If you're really worried about this, maybe I should... I don't know. I don't know."

I took her shoulders in my hands, my stomach tightening at the feel of her warm skin against my palms. "I've made you worried, and I'm sorry for that. I'm not going to lie and say there's nothing to be concerned about because that's just not me. But I'm also not about to blow smoke and tell you everything's fine when it's not. And for now, until we have more information, I think it is okay and continuing to be cautious is just smart."

Her dark brown eyes flickered back and forth between mine. "Why? I mean, why do you care?"

My pulse picked up a bit and I stepped closer, crowding her just a little. My fingers stroked along the slope of her neck and into the curve of her shoulder, sliding under the edge of the thin straps of her summery dress.

"I care, Em."

I'd already freaked her out enough, so I didn't plan to

make it worse. But I already felt protective of her. It was likely my fault if there was someone watching her. How they'd ID'd me as someone significant, we didn't know, but since we'd taught at the embassy and attended the gala, maybe that had been enough. And again, maybe we were missing something major or possibly, this was all nothing. But if someone was here and after her, it only made sense because they thought she was working with or for me.

Eyes locked, she licked her lips. "Okay, then."

"Simple as that, huh?"

She grinned. "Simple as that. Now please, feed me. I think my appetite just reappeared."

CHAPTER SIXTEEN

Emily

I had a text from West every day after work. We didn't
have cell communication at the office because it was a
secure facility, so I didn't see them until I powered on my
phone at the end of the day. Every time, my heart flipped.

They were simple things—questions about my day or
responses to my long list of things I wanted to know about
him. We went back and forth every evening.

Did he have any siblings? Yes, a much younger sister
still in college. Did I? Nope, only child.

Did he like to read? Yes, mostly news and political or
historical accounts of military action. Did I? Yes, give me all
the thrillers and romantic suspense.

Did he plan to stay in the Army indefinitely?

That one came with unspoken expectations in my own
mind, though I hoped they didn't register for him. I'd
mentioned my general disinterest in dating soldiers, but

clearly, he was different. And in many ways, he really was. He had stability here in ways most military personnel didn't have—he'd made clear he wouldn't be moving until retirement, and he was unlikely to move anywhere unless he joined his friends in some small town in Utah where they'd started a security company.

"I'll do my twenty and see how it's going. Only a few years left, though, and I hope to have good reasons to move on to whatever's next."

I wasn't brave enough to ask what those *good reasons* might be, but I related to this deeply. Not only did I want to leave Budapest for the next job, I wanted to have a reason to stay somewhere. I'd moved Stateside with the intention of staying here and finding those *good reasons* for myself.

Every bit of him he revealed called to me, and the more I learned, the more I saw him as regular-man Ryan, my friend and someone I liked a whole lot, and not the super-brained hero-soldier warrior who still seemed kind of unreal to me. More significantly, I saw him as someone I could see myself with—whose life, though I was only beginning to understand it, was something I might actually be open to sharing.

On Thursday of that week, a familiar voice came from the hallway outside my office. The low tone sent my heart racing, and I straightened my spine and quickly checked my teeth in my phone screen. *All clear.*

"Hey, Em. Have a minute?"

I startled and shoved the lip gloss I'd grabbed back into my purse and smiled over at him. *Dang,* the man was handsome. I hadn't forgotten, but seeing him leaning casually against the doorframe had an instant effect on me. All our chatting had made him feel so accessible and, for lack of a better word, soft. Welcoming of my questions and quick to return my jokes. But the reality of him was more than a little overwhelming. *So much for regular man.*

My breath rushed out and I stood. "Sure. Yeah. I was about to take lunch."

"Can I join you?" he said, a small smile on his face.

"Sure. Naomi and I had talked about sitting together, but she had to leave early. I guess her older son's sick." I couldn't imagine juggling adulthood and single parenting, but from what I'd learned about her, she was doing a great job of it.

"Naomi's great. I'm sorry Danny's sick though. I'll have South check in on her—they're neighbors." He chuckled at my surprise. "I told you, there are a lot of good people who live there."

"You convinced me. I have an appointment with a realtor soon." I was nervous to set down roots and be surrounded by people from work, but I also liked the idea of knowing my neighbors. I'd always gotten to know the people close by, but I'd never felt like I lived in a true community. Sunny Pines seemed to have that in spades. And honestly, hotel living was for the birds.

We bustled into the dining facility—easily the nicest I'd ever seen in my time working for the military—and each grabbed a tray. The food selection focused on lean meats, fish, steamed vegetables, complex carbs, and a few treats along with a huge selection at the salad and fruit bar. I'd been baffled by the whole thing and how upscale it all seemed compared to regular glops of mashed potatoes and gravy and overcooked burgers I'd seen in other DFACs, until my boss explained that fueling the operators was part of their upkeep and training. If they didn't have access to high-quality protein and the right fuel, they couldn't be expected to stay in peak physical condition.

Had my mind immediately flown to West in his T-shirt and how it'd stretched over the curves of his biceps and chest and grazed down the slight ripples of his abs at the barbecue?

Of course it had. I couldn't blame it. Even now, he had the sleeves of his plaid shirt rolled to his elbows and one glance at him holding his tray, the tendons flexed and his strong hands grasping the edges...

"Did you want to sit with the Cards?"

I dumped a spoonful of cubed watermelon onto my plate and glanced up at him, glad I hadn't actually been staring at his wrists during my little admiration session. Not that he seemed overtly egotistical, because he didn't. He didn't walk into a room and expect everyone to applaud or anything. It was more that he had such ground-level confidence, it was like gravity for him. I wasn't sure I wanted to add to it with my ogling his wrists.

"I'm good with whatever," I said, because I genuinely enjoyed his teammates, and I didn't mind meeting more of his colleagues.

The operators tended to eat in teams and all cozied up around the same tables, while the people who worked in basically every other job, from what I could tell, scattered around the rest of the space. It was a large room with a two-story atrium lined with glass that let sunlight in. Surprisingly ethereal considering the context of who worked here, but I'd also learned how many dignitaries and political leaders, including the president, came to visit, so they liked things to look nice.

To my surprise, West sat us near but not with his team.

"You didn't want to sit with them?" I asked as he scooted in my chair, then took his seat.

"I'm going to get plenty of them soon enough, and I'll be missing you."

He dove right into his meal, so I did, too, letting the warmth caused by his words wash over me.

And also a jump of surprise. Why did it feel like a big deal for him to say he'd miss me? Granted, I felt the same. We talked constantly outside of work thanks to our text threads, and these quick lunches were something that made me all kinds of floaty for the rest of the day. I was genuinely dreading him leaving. I liked my coworkers and I could make plans with Katie and Noah while he was gone, but the person I most wanted to talk to and see lately was him.

"You're leaving?" I asked after a few bites.

He nodded while he finished chewing. "We are. Not sure exactly when, but it'll likely be early next week. And on that note, I wanted to see if you'd join me for dinner this weekend."

I bought time by taking a drink, not sure why I needed to but needing a moment nonetheless. "When are you thinking?"

"Friday? Saturday works, too, if that's better."

"Hey, did you see Naomi? I thought she told me you two were having lunch together." South slid into the seat next to me and eyed my plate, then West's. When he reached for one of his carrots, West swatted the back of South's hand with his fork.

I covered my mouth to stifle the laugh as South scowled and said, "Sugar cookies!" in the same tone someone would say, "Ouch!"

"Didn't you just eat?" West asked.

South only shrugged a shoulder.

"Naomi had to leave. I think her oldest son is sick," I explained.

"Thanks. See you guys." And he was gone.

I looked at West. "Um... that seemed startlingly abrupt."

West grinned and his eyes flicked to what had to be South's retreating form behind me. "You'll learn soon enough that South is compulsively available for Naomi. And when you see them together, you'll understand why. Just don't say anything to her... it's a whole thing. Point is, you don't need to worry about Danny or Naomi. South's got them."

My heart squeezed for all of this... the idea that the big man had a soft spot for my new friend and her sons, and even the idea that he felt more and couldn't express it. I didn't know why she was a single mom, but I guessed South's choice to reserve his feelings had something to do with that.

Startlingly, I also felt a little bit of longing cut through me, but for what? For South? Definitely not. For West?

Yes. Maybe. *If we're being honest, then yes minus the maybe.*

But did I want his devotion, his attention, his time, his... heart? And amazingly, it seemed he was willing to give them to me—certainly his attention, time, and what felt like devotion. Despite being a badass soldier, he seemed surprisingly determined to woo me and spend time with me, to get to know me in small ways. It was a lot, but so far it felt like it was a lot in a good way.

And it made my doubts about him waver. Or, not doubts about *him*, but doubts about how this would work with him being in dangerous situations and my heart surviving if something happened to him... it made even that waver.

"So this weekend? Will you let me cook for you?"

West asked the question as though he didn't already

know the answer, but he had to. And I did, too, so I told him the truth, "Of course."

I hadn't been this nervous in a long time. Well, this *kind* of nervous, maybe. Because I'd been crazy nervous the night after I'd thought I'd seen the guy from Budapest, but so far, there'd been nothing. No more sightings, no developments. I'd been in touch with Lucinda about the symposium, and I'd gotten a few texts from József checking in and asking if I was still planning to come back for the event since I'd told him when I'd left that I'd see him again in a few weeks, but otherwise, all was quiet on the Budapest front. I'd mentioned the messages to West and he'd seemed understanding that it was part of my job to stay in touch—at least with Lucinda. Since no news was, well, no news, nothing seemed to have changed.

And thank goodness, because it left me enough energy to deal with the drinking-from-the-firehose effect of the new job learning curve and then... whatever this with West was. Exclusivity with a side of alpha male and a hint of *I barely know this guy* peppered with—well, that was enough, wasn't it?

What did he expect from me? What did he actually want from me? He was so straightforward it was almost hard to believe. It was just so different from anyone I'd ever dated. I'd known he would be, and yet here I was, my hands a little shaky as I approached his door and rang the bell.

And the more important question—what did I want from him? I liked him, but was I ready for all of his intensity? And more importantly, was I really ready to learn more about him and get closer to a man who would absolutely leave and run into danger? Who would be the person rescuing captives and hunting down bad guys and constantly in life-endangering peril? Him, surely. And he wouldn't hit twenty and be out anytime soon, from what I'd gathered. Did I have it in me to brave that limbo of uncertainty and live with my heart in my throat every time he stepped out of the house?

Less than a minute later, he answered looking so heart-stoppingly gorgeous, I forgot all of those worries and just took him in.

The brown hair and beard looking styled but not too manicured, the piercing blue of his eyes roaming all over me while I did the same for him. His button-down shirt was open at the top and I could see the dip of his throat, and he'd rolled up the sleeves of the navy material, showcasing his wrists. *Of course.*

"Come in. Glad you made it."

He gestured into the living room where I'd sat with him last weekend, and after closing the door behind me, led the way into the kitchen. It'd either been redone or just well done the first time, with gray cabinets and a dark farmhouse-style sink with dappled gray, white, and black marble or stone counters. Stainless steel appliances gave everything a sleek, updated look, but the thick wooden cutting board and a pot bubbling on the stove kept the scene from being too sterile.

"This is beautiful," I said, wondering how many of the homes in the area had kitchens like this. I by no means possessed the skills to make full use of a kitchen like this, but I did cook for myself more often than not. Maybe, with the right setup, I could channel my inner Summer Masters and *really* learn to cook.

Music played softly, something with words my mind couldn't quite latch onto, and my stomach did an odd combination of swooping and rumbling from hunger and affection. Don't ask me why thinking of Ryan West bustling around his kitchen cooking dinner for me to music painted such a vivid, alluring picture, but it did.

He'd become this larger-than-life thing to me over the years, and seeing him in stealth mode at the embassy dressed in a tux and charming the ambassador and Bri Williamson hadn't exactly helped things. Glimpsing his human side—hearing the music he chose to listen to, seeing a pile of mail tucked away, even remembering his less than perfect thread-bare shirt from the barbecue, had made me... well as much as it should've made me more comfortable, it kind of terrified me.

Logically, seeing he was a human man and not some idealized version of a super soldier was a good thing. I wouldn't want to actually date a super soldier anyway. I'd always said I didn't want *any* kind of soldier, hadn't I?

But that was the problem—if he wasn't a caricature, but an actual human man with feelings and faults and desires and struggles... well, crap. What hope did I have of resisting him?

"Thanks for coming. I figured we'd enjoy the privacy of eating in and then we're free to talk about anything." His blue eyes dipped to where my hands clutched a bottle of wine, then returned to my gaze. "You good?"

"Yes." I thrust the bottle at him. "This is for you. I wanted to bring something."

And wow, the nerves just kept coming. But he was so confident and in control and whatever he was cooking in his kitchen smelled so good it all just felt... honestly, it felt a little too good to be true, with a side of that same *he is an actual person* thinking that was really throwing me.

I wasn't a woman who had a hard time believing I deserved good things. But there was admittedly part of me that felt like this whole situation went far beyond good into the land of fairy tales, and I hadn't quite figured out how to reconcile the feeling. Paired with a genuine worry that this all felt too fast too soon and with the exact wrong kind of person—the kind I'd always thought I didn't want—and it left me more than a little mentally and emotionally adrift in his spacious, lovely kitchen.

"Thank you. You didn't have to bring anything, but that's thoughtful." He took the bottle, our fingers grazing and sending a thrill from the tiny point of contact all the way up my arm.

"Of course. Thank you for inviting me."

I saw his smile before he turned to place the bottle on the counter and then moved over to the stove to check whatever was cooking.

"I should've asked you what you like to eat, but I figured since it was rainy and gross, I'd make us soup—beef stew." He took a small silver spoon and scooped up a bit of the liquid, tasted it, then nodded to himself and set the spoon in the sink. "Want to try?"

"Sure." I moved toward him, willing my pulse to slow and this sense of unsure shyness to abate.

He dipped another spoon in, then held it out to me, one hand cupped underneath to catch spills. And rather than take the utensil and risk spilling it, I grasped his wrist and leaned forward, slipping the end of the spoon into my mouth.

"Wow, that's great. Is this a recipe you make often?" I

asked, eager to have more because it really was the perfect thing for this weirdly chilly, rainy North Carolina evening. From what I'd seen, we needed to savor this cooler weather before it heated up again for summer and never looked back.

"It's a go-to for sure. I'm sorry it's nothing fancier. I'm a pretty simple man and my food reflects that." He ladled soup into two bowls, then moved to a cutting board and sliced into a large boule of crusty bread.

"I'm pretty sure I have to call you on that. You are not a simple man."

He tossed me a look over his shoulder as he loaded slices of bread onto the plates he'd set the bowls on. "What makes you say that?"

"You speak five languages fluently."

He carried the plates to the dining table, where two places were set with dark place mats on top of a blond wood table.

"That's just something about me. It's not who I am."

I chuckled. "Sure. But you're an EMU operator, right? That is not simple."

Some part of me begged for all of this to be something I couldn't handle—for *him* to be this complex person I didn't want. But every bit of him he revealed only made those objections over his work feel alarmingly flimsy.

He pulled out my chair, and I slid into the seat across from him.

"That's my job," he said, but he gave me a sly look and a raised brow.

I shook my head. "Sure. Just your job. Not a fundamental part of you after doing the job for, what, over a decade?"

He gave me that with a tip of his head. "Fair enough. It's a pretty all-encompassing job. It becomes life."

Exactly. That was the reality of any military job because it required the world to collapse around the servicemember to some degree, and in special operations, it seemed all the more true. That wasn't even touching the dangerous realities of the things he did while deployed.

He squinted a little and took a bite of soup. We ate quietly for a moment, my thoughts swirling around his admission and this sense that even such honesty from him appealed to me, before he continued.

"That's the thing, though. That's what I'm growing tired of."

I chewed a piece of the delicious crusty bread while thinking about his statement, an odd mix of doom and hope churning in my chest. After a sip of wine he'd opened, I asked, "The job? Or the nature of it?"

"Honestly? Maybe a little of both. I'm not done yet, but I feel the wear and tear more now than I used to. Takes me longer to recover from injuries or when things go wrong. But more than that..." His gaze tipped up from where it'd focused on his soup to meet mine, his blue eyes full of feeling as he continued. "It's the way I've prioritized it. I'm ready to let more into my life."

I swallowed hard. "More."

"Yes, Emily. And forgive me for being direct, but you're someone who makes me want that. You're contributing to the problem, really."

A shocked laugh tripped out of me, and he grinned. He shouldn't be able to throw that smile around without a license or at least some sort of early warning system because *wow*, his smile was nothing short of devastating. Defenses dropped, will to resist his charms annihilated, especially in the wake of his disarming honesty.

"Please explain to me how I'm contributing to your problem."

He set down his spoon and leaned an elbow on the table, then pinned me with his crystalline blue gaze.

"Because you're the one who started it. I never felt that until I met you in Germany. And now that you're here, it's not a question. I'm not wondering whether I do want more, whether I could find someone to have it with. It's certain. I do want more, and I want to know if you're the person to have it with."

CHAPTER SEVENTEEN

West

Well, I pushed her, and as though her mission tonight aimed at showing me exactly who she was, she pushed right back.

Damn, but I liked this about her. It wasn't simply that she wasn't bowled over by my honesty. She didn't hide the fact that my desire for a future with someone and my curiosity about whether *she* was that someone proved overwhelming. After my little speech during dinner, she'd shaken her head and ate some more soup, buying herself time.

She didn't avoid responding, though. Instead, she ended up nodding to herself after a few seconds like she'd decided something, and then she said, "That's intense, but I get it. I don't want to waste time or play games."

And from there, we'd kept talking. We shifted to her work and her time as a GS employee for so long. She mentioned how getting away from education centers had challenged her, and how hard the year in Budapest had been but how grateful she was for it. She'd be returning there to deal with one last project, which I didn't love, but it also wasn't exactly my call. Plus, hopefully soon we'd have everything going wrong there righted.

After that, we turned to movies we liked, favorite recipes, other things we did in our spare time. She liked to read, I liked to get outside. She'd always wanted a cat, and I'd never had an animal, because I'd always hated the idea of leaving it alone or having to ask a neighbor for help whenever we blew out on mission.

We settled on the couch to talk and sip wine until we both switched to water. I lit a fire in the fireplace, and when I walked back to the couch and saw her snuggled into the corner with her feet tucked under her, my heart squeezed.

This night had been so simple and perfect, and soon, she'd have to leave. As sure as I was that Emily meant something to me already and I wanted more from her, I wouldn't rush anything between us. My honesty wasn't supposed to be some kind of seduction technique, and though I wouldn't mind getting closer to her, I didn't want to do anything to make her feel like I couldn't be patient and wait for her to catch up.

Her eye snagged on my phone when it lit up with an incoming text. "Oh, gosh, I didn't realize how late it is. I should go."

I pocketed the phone knowing I'd deal with whatever had come through in the message in a few minutes and stood, holding out a hand to her. She accepted, setting her small, soft hand in mine.

Heat and pleasure radiated out from where our palms

pressed and fingers laced. When was the last time I'd held hands with a woman like this?

It'd been years, and certainly longer since I'd felt as invested in someone as I did now. Maybe this made me a fool considering it was only our second date, and yet it felt like we'd shared so much. We'd met years ago, and our interactions in Budapest had been charged.

She'd kept my secret. She'd kept *me* safe.

This truth had settled into my bones over the last few weeks, and nothing progressing between us had changed the certainty. I'd felt safe with my team, my friends, but I'd never been with a woman who made me feel it. Desired, yes. Interesting or admirable, sure. But safe?

I hadn't considered how valuable such a truth would be until I had it with Emily. She knew the reality of my life— that I was in the EMU, yes, but even one of my cover names. And she'd done nothing to leverage or abuse this knowledge. I was thankful for this in the most obvious sense that it allowed my team to accomplish what we needed that night in Budapest and in the time after, but I was also immensely grateful to find she hadn't wanted to use it for any purpose. She'd wanted to understand, of course, but even now, she hadn't pushed.

Working for EMU had clarified for her the limitations of what I could share, no doubt, but still. More than that one instance, more and more, I felt sure I could trust her with more than just my job and my name.

All of that was logical. The other aspect here was this pull toward her, this need to touch her and hold her and make her feel pleasure and joy like I'd never known. It was hanging on what words she'd say next and reining in the suspicion that this woman was it for me. As if knowing I could trust her opened the floodgates of my heart and also, I suspected more and more, my soul.

None of that was logical and yet, here it was, an arrow flying for a target I never saw coming from a bow I didn't know I'd flexed.

"Thank you for coming tonight. I hope we can do it again soon," I said, turning to face her before I opened the door.

"Thanks for having me," she said, then did that thing where she must've internally been talking to herself and added, "You're not going to try to convince me to stay longer?"

I grinned and dropped her hand, then dared to settle my palms on the dip of her waist above the band of her jeans. "If I did, would you stay?"

She huffed even though she was grinning. "Not tonight, no."

I chuckled softly. "I figured. And so I'm not going to shoot my shot just yet."

"But you plan to at some point?" she asked, letting her hands come to rest on my chest.

Stepping closer, I ducked my head and urged her closer with my hands. "Definitely."

And then, because I could no longer resist the pull of her, I closed the distance between us, mouth seeking hers as I drew her flush with me. Her hands trailed up my chest and neck and into my hair within seconds of the contact, like she'd been waiting for me to do this all night.

This evidence suggested I shouldn't have waited, but it was also ideal. She not only wanted to kiss me but we were on the same page—we'd get to more, much more, just not tonight.

When she angled her head to deepen the kiss, I groaned and backed her into the wall. This was so much better than our almost-kiss in Budapest when I thought I'd never see her again.

The tether banded around my self-control began to slip as she eagerly met each slide and touch of my lips and tongue with her own. Her nails dragged along my scalp, and the combination of sensations had a dizzying effect I never wanted to end.

But end, it must. And the buzz of my phone reminded me of this in a cruel jolt to my back pocket. I broke the kiss and gazed at her hazy expression clearing.

"Time to go," she said, sliding her hands from my hair and letting them drop to her sides.

I nodded and very reluctantly stepped back, away from her warmth and softness. "Let me know when you get to your room."

And ten minutes later, her text came through telling me she was tucked into her room safe. By then, I'd volleyed a dozen messages back and forth with the guys and I'd started packing.

Most likely, we'd fly out Wednesday, but there was a chance the schedule could change and we'd need to be ready. All the more reason I was glad Emily had come over. I'd be gone for at least a week, maybe slightly more, and after that, I'd be back for a nice stretch while another squadron took the active missions.

I didn't want to wait until after this to move forward with her, or to be unsure whether I could anticipate seeing her when I got back. She wasn't as certain as I was that she wanted something long term and committed. I could see it, and she wasn't hiding the fact that my intensity about all this was a lot. But it gave me hope she was considering what I was saying with care, not brushing it off.

Or so I very much hoped.

So far, so good, though. She'd wanted to stay even though she knew she wouldn't. She was glad I wanted the same. And she didn't seem to mind the kissing...

I could come home to her. Not in the way that was settling into my chest and making me ache with a longing I wasn't used to, but at least to continue where we left off.

Now I had genuine reason to hope this would grow into more. And I just needed her to catch up.

CHAPTER EIGHTEEN

Emily

I slept surprisingly well considering how buzzy and excited I was when I got back to my hotel room the night before. Spending time with Ryan West was at once exciting and relaxing and exhilarating. It was already extremely comfortable, and maybe all the reasons he'd named for why he was taking things seriously and slowly were the same ones that made me feel at home with him.

At home. The thought struck me as I turned into Sunny Pines to meet my realtor and look for my own home. Did I really feel that comfortable with him?

Not at first. Not when I'd walked into his lovely home and been nearly awestruck by how honest to goodness attractive I found him *and* the news that not only was the man smart-hot and hot-hot, but also capable-hot. I mean, of course he was capable as an operator, but he could also cook. Really well. Sure, maybe soup isn't the hardest thing, but it was a delicious vegetable beef that'd been rib-sticking without being heavy. It'd been comforting and the perfect thing for a cozy night in after a chilly, rainy day.

Oof, I liked this man. My first thought was to think I liked him *too much*, but I'd stopped short of that in the last few hours. Maybe I didn't like him too much—maybe it was just the right amount. He certainly seemed to like me, too, and so why hide away from those feelings when we'd both acknowledged our desire to see where this went?

Wasn't this how dating worked? And yes, he seemed certain of things in a way I didn't understand or feel yet, but there was nothing wrong with moving forward. I was enjoying spending time with him and I was being honest about my feelings and that I was open to his book but not exactly on the same page.

Although every text and minute spent together put me closer to his page, far faster than I could've anticipated.

My realtor waved at me with a huge helping of enthusiasm from the driveway of the home I'd inquired about last week. We'd met before since I'd seen a few houses in other places during my first few weeks here, but nothing had stuck. I wasn't hugely picky, but it did help to see a variety, and I'd told her I wasn't ready to rush into anything. I owned a small home that a rental company managed for me back at Fort Campbell, and since then, I'd been renting or living in government-furnished housing, so I had no desire to force a buy.

This house was a few blocks from West's house, so at least I wouldn't be in his back yard or anything. I didn't know where the other Cardinals lived, but South had to be somewhere around here since I'd seen him jogging a street over. I was fairly certain North lived here, too.

"Hello, hello, Emily! Are we ready to see your future home?"

"Let's see how it goes!"

My realtor waved as she sped away to her next appointment. She'd apologized profusely for having to run, but I preferred it this way. I didn't want to be talked into anything. I liked the house a lot, but I wasn't quite ready to make an offer. She warned me it likely wouldn't last long on the market, and I could see why. It had all the things I wanted, and the location, as I was quickly learning, was incredibly desirable.

I just... wasn't ready. This was huge for me, and I wanted to be sure.

"You looking at this one?" Naomi asked as she approached on the sidewalk.

"Oh my gosh, hi!" I bent to wave at one boy teetering on a bicycle with training wheels and another in the stroller she pushed.

"This is Danny and that's Benny. Boys, can you say hi to Miss Emily?" Naomi asked.

"Hi, Miss Emily," Danny said clearly from his precarious seat atop the bike.

"Hi, Missy," Benny pronounced.

I chuckled and grinned at Naomi, who was smiling down at the boys. "Can I walk with you all? I thought I might get a feel for the neighborhood."

"That'd be perfect. Did you like the inside?" she asked as we strolled slowly behind Danny.

We chatted about the features I did like and a few things I wasn't sure about like the dusty pink tiles in the guest bathroom, which hadn't been remodeled, and the knowledge that I'd have to replace the AC units in the near term. I didn't particularly want to move in somewhere that needed a lot of work, because I wasn't handy beyond basic things like fixing a running toilet and patching up drywall, and I didn't want to feel uprooted by renovations.

"I can say I've lived in this neighborhood for three years and I love it. I'm so grateful we ended up here." She smiled at me, but it dropped instantly when she sucked in a breath at the sight of something over my shoulder.

"What—" *Oh.*

A line of jogging men four across rapidly approached where we stood, each shirtless and glistening in the sun.

That's right, glistening.

My stomach dropped right along with my jaw as I took in the absolute majesty of the image as they gained ground toward us.

Naomi made a garbled sound, then sighed.

"That's..." I searched for the word.

"My favorite view. Forgive me for saying it, but I mean..." She widened her eyes at me and we cracked up, laughing at the moment.

"Hey, ladies!" South shouted as they got closer, then slowed to a walk about ten feet from us.

"Scotty!" Danny hopped off his bike and bolted into the street toward South. The giant of a man lunged toward him and scooped him up instantly.

"Hey, buddy. You can't run into the road, right?" South said, talking quietly to the little boy in his arms.

"I know, but you catched me."

South said something else I couldn't hear right as West, North, and East stepped up onto the sidewalk.

"Out for a light jog today, gentlemen?" I asked, simply delighted to find my voice sounding normal and not ragged with thirst for the man leaning in to plant a kiss on my cheek.

"We did a quick ten. It's been a while since we've done any distance," North said, bending over to tie a loose shoelace and giving us all an eyeful of his butt in his running shorts.

I jerked my gaze away and laughed as I caught West's eye and noticed East shaking his head with his hands on his hips.

South approached us and I realized Naomi was helping Benny out of the stroller, her cheeks bright with a blush as Danny said, "You're all sweaty."

"I am. I just ran a long way really fast." South opened his mouth like this was the most incredible thing, and Danny giggled.

"How fast were you?" Danny asked, grabbing South's face on either side.

"Did you like the house?" West asked, ducking his head to capture my attention away from Danny and South.

I'd been trying not to pay too much attention to him and his chest of wonders, but I'd seen enough to know he had more than a six-pack, a chest that looked carved from marble, and that dip at his hips that turned me into a far less sophisticated woman than I normally was.

My gaze dropped to said chest despite my staunch directive to stick to his face, and my cheeks heated before I bounced back to meet his eyes. "Um, the house. Yes. The house. It was... good."

He squinted at me. "So good you can hardly form a sentence about it, huh?"

I cleared my throat and glanced back at Naomi and her boys. "I may be a touch distracted."

His smirking face greeted me when I dared look back at him.

"Really? By what?"

I blinked at him, only a little charmed by his fake obliviousness. "By how cute South is being with the boys, of course."

His full-out grin had me huffing out a breath, but his warm hand settled on my arm and drew every bit of my attention to him.

"Can you still come over?"

We'd already talked about hanging out again today. I'd mentioned my appointment and he'd said I should stop by. I'd planned to text him when I was done, but then the whole jogging situation happened.

"I can, if you're free." My traitorous eyes slipped over him again.

"I'm sorry I'm just getting back. I was thinking you'd be with the realtor longer. If you can give me five minutes, I'll run home and hop into the shower and be ready for you."

Ryan West. In the shower. Ready for me.

No. Nooo. That's not what he means.

I coughed to cover any other kind of sound I might've made at the thought of such a scene. "That's great. I'll be over in five or more."

He squeezed my arm and hollered a goodbye to South. North and East joined him in what seemed like a very fast run, after offering me and Naomi nods goodbye.

Naomi sighed as we both watched them run. It was sort of like watching the Clydesdales with their movement so in sync, but they weren't beautiful horses. They were exceptionally beautiful men.

"I guess South is going to carry them both back—oh, and the bike..." she trailed off as South bent down to snatch up Danny's bike with one hand while somehow balancing Danny in his upper arm.

Naomi pushed the empty stroller ahead of us. South now held Danny and his bike with one arm and Benny in the other. The beast of a man threw his head back and laughed, then started jogging lightly with the two boys.

I caught Naomi's eye before she turned and mouthed, "Wow" and she shook her head and silently said, "I know."

"Is he always like this with them?" I asked, marveling at how comfortable he seemed. It wasn't that I didn't believe men could be good with kids, more than I didn't know many who were naturally so at ease when they didn't have children of their own.

She didn't respond for a moment, her gaze following the little scene, then sighed with what sounded like defeat. "He is."

"Is that a bad thing?" I was new in town, so there could be a lot I didn't understand about the situation.

"Oh, it's good for a lot of reasons. But..." She shook her head and offered me a sad smile. "It gets to me."

Right as I was about to follow up on that statement, she stopped me with "I better catch up to them. See you soon, okay? Have fun with West." She wiggled her brows, then shuffled after them.

I wandered back to my car and waved as I passed them, rolling at a crawl as they all made their way back to what must've been Naomi and South's street. It would be pretty dreamy to live in this little neighborhood and see friends or walk around and see familiar faces.

The thought of familiar faces reminded me of seeing the man from Budapest. It's not like I'd forgotten about it. I'd refused to obsess about whether or not it had been that man. According to West, they couldn't reasonably say anyone had come here that they were tracking, but this didn't necessarily mean it hadn't been the man I'd thought. Then again, maybe it'd all been in my head.

Ugh, I'd gone around and around about it a thousand times by now. Thankfully, work had been all-consuming enough to distract me, and being close with West had given me a genuine sense of safety and connection, too.

My phone buzzed with a text as I parked in West's driveway, and when I checked, I was happy to see one from József. I sent him a quick response wishing him well, then made my way to West's front door. I wasn't nervous, exactly, but the anticipation of seeing him again after last night and, frankly, the confrontation with just exactly how fit he was, had my hands a little tingly with awareness.

I'd given him more like eight minutes since he'd run off, so I hoped that'd been enough time. If not, I could wander around his street a little and come back.

He didn't leave me waiting, though. Instead, he pulled open the door with jeans slung low on his hips, his hand running through his hair, which consequently showcased the ridiculous muscles of his biceps, and of course, no shirt because he was clearly trying to murder me.

Who needed to worry about threats from afar when I had this man in my life?

CHAPTER NINETEEN

West

She didn't respond the first time I invited her in. Her gaze had traveled a lazy, almost dreamlike route over my shoulders and chest, all the way down to my bare feet and back up. Her attention felt like fingertips dragging over my skin, and heat whipped through me.

I hadn't minded the way she was clearly affected by me earlier, and it certainly didn't bother me now. After all, if she answered the door in something less than fully clothed, I would likely have a similar response.

But for now, I wanted her inside, with more privacy than my doorstep offered, where I could touch her and talk to her and soak up a few more hours before the week ran away with us and the Cards and I had to take off. It was a nice neighborhood, but I had some nosy neighbors and no desire to spend another second holding back with her.

"Em? Want to come in?"

Her gaze snapped to meet mine. "What? Yes. Of course. Sorry. Yes."

I chuckled and widened the door further but only inched back when she stepped inside. Once she was clear of the door and standing directly in front of me, eyes locked on mine, I shut it with a push, then bent to kiss her.

She responded immediately with hands on my shoulders as I slid mine to her lower back, then farther down, and hoisted her up. She jumped and I lifted, and soon, her legs were locked around my waist and our kiss had gone from *It's good to see you* to *Stay the night, stay forever.*

Her hands slipped into my wet hair, and I moved so I could pin her against the wall and devour her properly. As always, she met me move for move with a dizzying give and take that had need coursing throughout every part of me.

After some amount of time, she broke the kiss, shaking her head and eyeing me.

"You are dangerous," she said, breath coming fast like she was the one who'd just finished a run.

I laughed. "I can say the same for you."

I released her slowly so her legs lowered to the ground, but I didn't back all the way off.

Her hands stayed planted on my skin, the connection between us still burning bright. With a sigh, she leaned her head against the wall and let her arms fall to her sides. I stepped back and grabbed her hand, pulling in a deep breath to calm my racing heart.

"Let's get comfortable and you can tell me about the house."

Five minutes later, we were sitting on the couch with glasses of icy water perched on coasters next to us on the coffee table, and she'd listed her favorite parts of the tour with the realtor.

She took a drink after finishing, but my mind was ticking away. Something didn't click about the way she was talking, but I couldn't quite put my finger on it.

"You seem reluctant to say you like it... or maybe that you don't like it. I can't quite tell which way you're leaning."

We were angled toward each other on the couch, each leaning an elbow on the back so we were facing the other, and therefore, no, she couldn't escape from my eye contact.

She wasn't evasive, exactly, but she could be cagey. I cherished every bit of her she let me see, and though it came in a slow release, we were getting there.

"Why am I hesitating?" she said, eyes tracking around the room—to the pile of mail on a side table next to my keys and wallet, the two outdoors magazines on the coffee table, the flat-screen TV my sister had insisted I program to show a large art piece rather than a black screen last time we'd video called.

"I've been trying to figure that out. I think..." She jolted as though clarity hit her. "I think in the back of my mind, buying a house again—one I plan to stay in and not rent when I move away—signals the end of my life as I've been living it. It's me saying I'm ready for something different in this really intense way and it's... a lot."

My hand covered her knee, and her eyes found mine. I felt no judgment for her, no criticism of the feelings she'd shared. Only a kind of odd kinship as I, too, sensed major changes coming, and also the need to comfort her.

"It's okay to mourn that change. Not that you need me to tell you that, but I guess I just want to say it's okay. You can feel however you need to feel about it, and if that means this house isn't the one, then it's not. You don't even have to buy a house if you decide you don't want to."

She swallowed hard and tears limned her eyes. Mine

widened at the sight and I surged forward, cupping her cheeks.

"You going to cry on me, Wender?" I said, originally planning on joking to shake her from the flood of emotions but ultimately just speaking softly.

"Maybe," she eked out.

I leaned in and pressed a kiss to her forehead, then wrapped her in a hug. Holding her right here was so much of what I wanted, it nearly choked me, but I let her go when she pulled back, swiping under her eyes to banish the tracks of tears that'd snuck out.

"Okay, I'm done with that. I don't even know why I'm crying about it." She shook her head, and a slight flush rose to her cheeks like she might be embarrassed for the show of emotion.

No surprise. Generally, Emily was composed and sturdy. She was even-keeled and I doubted many people saw her get emotional, let alone cry. That I had tonight wasn't lost on me.

"It's a lot of change. International move, unexpected job change, buying a house—any one of those would be huge." She was dealing with so much, I hated the idea that she'd add frustration with herself into the mix.

"Well... can we get you to cry? Or are you one of those men who never do?" she asked, voice still a little watery.

I grinned and stole a quick kiss, heart flipping at the way she used humor to ease herself out of the heavier moment. "I am not particularly emotional. Pretty steady, over all, though I'm not opposed to tears. It's not a thing I try to avoid, I just don't typically end up crying."

She sighed and rolled her eyes. "Of course not. Although, honestly, if you were also like, a beautiful crier with perfect little tears slipping down your cheeks as your blue eyes just got magically bluer, I'd probably have to protest."

A laugh rocked me back, and I covered my eyes with one hand and squeezed her arm with the other. When I settled, I asked, "You know you're a little odd, right?"

She beamed, then sobered instantly. "I hope that's not news to you, West, because I am likely far weirder than you even realize, and I hate the idea that we're going to keep this up just for you to be disappointed with my oddities."

My hand brushed over her cheek and tucked a fall of hair over her ear. Gaze flickering between her eyes, I wanted to make sure she heard me and believed me.

"Oh, Em. I can't wait to learn about them all."

Three days later, I'd spent as much time as I could with Emily—dinner twice and a lunch date in the cafeteria on two of the days as well. We'd talked late into the day on Sunday and into the night each time she came over for dinner. I'd narrowly avoided asking her to stay the night every time.

Some part of me felt maybe I liked her too much. Yes, things had moved quickly, but we had history. That said, I worried that maybe my lack of experience with real relationships was leading me to take things too seriously. At the same time, I desperately wanted to leave for this mission feeling certain.

Certain of *what*, I didn't know.

So when Em opened her door late on Wednesday night, concern in her eyes, I rushed inside.

"Is everything okay?" she asked.

Hugging her to me, I inhaled the scent of her shampoo and reveled in the feel of her. I'd grown far too attached to this woman, and a part of me I'd never experienced had awakened these last few weeks.

"We're leaving in a few hours. I just wanted to see you before I go," I said. She smiled and her eyes lit up like this news made her happy, but the furrow in her brow had me asking, "What's wrong?"

"I guess you can't really tell me how long you'll be gone, right?"

I exhaled, another new sensation gripping me. I'd never wanted to tell anyone the details of our travel or of a mission. Not until now. But for the success of the operation and the security of everyone involved, I couldn't, even as much as I trusted her already. I would never stop appreciating the reality that I did trust her, felt safe to be honest about my life as much as I could with her, but I still couldn't violate operational security.

"Not in detail. It'll depend on a few things, but it should only be a few weeks." Hopefully, a matter of days in truth, but I figured overshooting and returning sooner was better than having it stretch out unexpectedly and then making her worry.

From what we could tell, there may well be a new mole, or a second one, at the embassy in Budapest. Where we thought we'd shut things down, someone had stepped in and picked up where Gordon had dropped off. Being on-site would help fish them out, and since we'd done a good deal of ground work, we knew what we were looking for now.

"Will you be able to stay in touch at all?" She laced our fingers together and stared down at our linked hands.

Such a sweet, simple gesture had my heart pounding. What was wrong with me?

"Not likely, unfortunately. We tend to go dark for short-term things like this. I'll try to check in whenever I can, though."

Her lashes fluttered like she was absorbing this, then she nodded. "Okay. Is there anything I can do? To help you or... make things easier?"

I reached for my back pocket. "I should've asked you this sooner and I'm sorry I'm only mentioning it now. If you want, you could stay at my place."

Her mouth dropped open and nothing came out, so I continued. "I hope it doesn't seem like too much, but I was just thinking about how wasteful it is for you to be paying for a hotel when you could be there. I'll be gone, so you'll have it to yourself. You'll get a feel for the neighborhood and you can water my plant."

She chuckled. "Your plant?"

"Yeah, Arthur. He likes to be talked to and prefers watering every three days."

The smile on her face spread slowly, a sparkle of delight and genuine pleasure entering her expression in a way that sent my stomach tumbling.

"Well... I'd love to. I'm spread out here, as you can see" —she gestured around her—"but I'd really appreciate that, especially since I'll be traveling next week. And I will follow any directions you give me for Arthur."

I cupped her face, drawn to her, wanting her so much I could hardly think straight. "We need to talk about your trip, but for now..."

We were on the same page, her lips melding with mine and sending a bolt of both relief and longing through me. The seconds of our kiss unraveled into minutes, and if it hadn't been for my alarm, I doubted I would've had the strength to leave.

She spoke first, though, her voice quiet enough to be a whisper. "Do you get scared?"

I'd never thought about this part—about leaving someone behind. My friends who were married talked about leaving their spouses and kids with varying degrees of emotion, but it'd always seemed so far off to me. Standing here with her, seeing the genuine concern and maybe even an edge of fear in her gaze, I wanted to do whatever I could to allay her worry.

"No. Not really. I get focused. I trust my team, my command, and the plans we've made. It doesn't mean things don't go wrong, because they do. It doesn't mean bad things don't happen, because they have. But it means I know my best chance of accomplishing the mission is staying in a place where my mind is crystal clear and my objectives are in sight. Anticipation keeps me moving, and then it's a kind of calm execution mode when we really dive in."

She shook her head, lips soft and open enough I had to claim them, taste them again. My alarm strummed an encore, jarring us apart.

"I'm so sorry, but I have to go."

She brushed a hand through my hair and cupped my cheek, then pressed a kiss to my lips. "No apologies. Go do your hero thing and then come back to me."

"I will. But wait, your trip. Where are you going next week?"

"Budapest. I think I mentioned a women's symposium I've been planning—that's next week."

My heart sank before I could stop it. For some reason I thought she had a stateside TDY next week and there was more time until her Budapest trip—how had I gotten that wrong? "Back to Budapest, huh? Please be careful. I'm hearing things."

She blinked. "Should I be concerned?"

"You should stay at your hotel or the embassy. Try not to go anywhere alone. Do all the things you know to do, but double it."

Head shaking, she huffed. "Sure, easy. Run a high-profile event with internationally recognized women speaking and attending and do all that."

Gathering her to me, I pressed a kiss to her head, her temple. "The nature of the event will help. Keep your eyes open though, okay? And no coincidences."

She swallowed but nodded. "Okay."

"And I'd say let's not have any one-on-ones with your Hungarian buddy or anyone else who isn't working at the embassy, yeah?"

Her head tilted to the side like she didn't hear me right. "As in József?"

"Yes, as in József."

She squinted. "I was going to see him."

My jaw flexed. "Really."

"Yes."

"You're going out with him?" Damn, that wasn't the point, but I couldn't help the ridiculous flicker of jealousy this inspired in me.

I'd earned the glare she gave me. Jealousy for *no reason* at a time like this was awful, but trying to convince her of anything by acting like I was her team leader and not her boyfriend wasn't likely to win me any points either.

"No. Not a date. A chance to catch up with a friend before I'm gone from Europe indefinitely. I have nothing but friendly feelings for him, or I wouldn't have agreed to exclusively date you."

"Right. I apologize for insinuating otherwise. That said, you shouldn't see him."

She inhaled slowly, as though she needed to calm herself. "Why not?"

"I'm telling you, Em, it's not smart. He checked out okay, as you know, but something's off about all of this, and until we know what, or until more time passes and we can see everything's okay, you should stay away from him and anyone else who's not from the embassy."

She exhaled, still working to steady herself, before speaking. "I appreciate that you're trying to help me, but at the risk of sounding like I'm saying *you're not the boss of me,* I'm going to make my own choices on this."

"That's your right, but I hope you'll factor in my decade-plus career in reading situations like this and—"

"You're right. I guess I just don't like feeling like my life is impacted by whatever this is, but then I think of the women who were taken, and of course it is. Theirs certainly was, in a way I can't imagine. I'm not used to having someone else dictate rules to me."

I nodded, deeply grateful for her understanding. "I'm not trying to tell you what to do or dictate anything."

She nodded slowly, clearly thinking through something. "Do you think if I make sure it's at the hotel where there'll be extra security, and make sure I'm with other people at all times, that would cover the bases?"

My jaw ticked and my mind spun. I wanted to say no. *No.* Just don't see this guy and stay safe and don't do anything that will put you at risk. But in theory, being at the hotel should mean heightened security for her, the speakers, and everyone attending. She wasn't about to go put herself in danger to spite me, but fear clawed at my throat as I said, "If you have to, that'd be best. I'm just asking you to be safe. Work with me here."

Her gaze shuttered, the openness that'd been there slipping away by the second. "Right. I am working with you in that I'm trying to find a way that fits with my own life and addresses your concerns. I'm saying I will be safe. Your question and my answer *do* have bearing on our future together. I appreciate you sharing your perspective and concern and also what you think is best."

I grumbled a little. "To be clear, what I think is best is to not see him at all and just focus on the symposium."

Her face was so, so serious when she said, "Ryan, I want to be clear. I care about you, but this is a lot."

"Me trying to make sure you're safe is a lot?"

Her lips thinned and clearly, I'd said the wrong thing, or maybe I just hadn't understood at all. For that matter, I didn't understand this.

"I'm not someone who can just fold into whatever you say. And I don't mean to say I don't hear your word of warning. I just—" She swallowed hard, frustration seeping into her tone. "I can't just surrender everything I am when you have an opinion."

Stunned, I scrambled for the right words to diffuse this. "I don't want that. I'm not asking you to."

"It feels like it. I'm not trying to be difficult. And I'm going to be smart. You can trust that, right?"

"I guess you're right." What else could I say? How had this gotten so off course?

"I am. I always am."

Her hint of a lopsided smile loosened the coiled-tight sensation in my chest an inch or two. "We'll see about that."

Our gazes caught and I wanted to kiss her again but felt like I should let her choose how this parting went. I'd bungled this conversation, or she had, or more likely we both had. We'd gone from being sad to say goodbye to this strained tension where I'd apparently stepped all over her, and I hadn't meant to. I just wanted her safe.

She nodded as though we'd come to the end of things. "Okay. Have a good trip. Stay safe."

"You, too." I stepped toward the door, longing to touch her, kiss her, hold her to me for a while until this push between us resolved into a pull. "See you soon, Em."

Stay safe, I almost said again, but instead, I left, leaving her to her space, to believe that I trusted her instead of continuing to push what I thought was best. And praying she'd be okay.

I hated leaving her, but I would be back. Back to her, as soon as I could. And I prayed she'd heed my warning, or that said warning proved unnecessary. I prayed the mission I was about to take on not far from Budapest wouldn't have anything to do with her.

CHAPTER TWENTY

Emily

In some ways, it felt like six months or more since I'd left Budapest, and in others, it'd been the blink of an eye.

In truth, it'd been about eight weeks. Stepping back into the US embassy after a mediocre night's sleep in a decent hotel not far from the historic building where I'd worked for a year felt surprisingly normal.

"Emily, good to see you. Are you prepared?" Lucinda's imperious tone welcomed me, her patent tablet-toting pose greeting me as warmly as ever.

"That I am, Lucinda. It's going to be an amazing event." I believed that, and clearly, she did, too, since her only response was a curt drop of her chin and purse of her lips before she turned and scuttled off.

I checked with the local venue where we'd be hosting the event, a gorgeous hotel a few blocks away nestled right on the Danube. This allowed the speakers to stay there or nearby and provided more event space since our largest rooms were far more intimate than the ballrooms offered at the hotel.

My phone buzzed with a text, and I checked to find a greeting from József. We'd planned to get coffee at some point before I'd talked to West, though I'd kept it vague while traveling. West clearly didn't want me to, and honestly, I hated that I'd had this gut-level pushback when he'd said it.

He was being protective. It wasn't like that came as news to me. He'd been that way from the very start, and he'd never liked József, even after he'd clarified that he wasn't a red flag. Logically, I understood he was being cautious, and I should appreciate this and not feel hemmed in by his suggestions.

But that was just it—he was most likely trying to protect me from nothing. They'd vetted József before and if he'd been a problem, I would've known about it by now. He'd been a decent friend to me and I liked the idea of one last coffee to wish him well, one more thing to put a bow on my time here. It couldn't actually be rooted in jealousy for Ryan, but it almost felt like it—some alpha-hole version of keeping me safe that meant keeping me away from other men. But he had no reason to doubt me on this, no reason to believe I'd want József, and ultimately, not trusting *him*.

Still, the person I supposedly saw in North Carolina had never shown up again, and the further from the incident I got, the more I was convinced it was all in my stress-addled jet-lagged head.

At the same time, I hated the idea of West worrying. I also knew that just because something didn't seem like a threat to me, didn't mean it wasn't one. And if this man who clearly cared about me was asking me to be cautious, wasn't that the least I could do for him *and* myself?

I cringed thinking about our last conversation—how I'd just let him leave without hugging or kissing him goodbye. A thought clawed at me—what if something happened to him? I was less worried about *me*, but still… what if I'd been so scared of how much he cared about me and the fact that in my gut I knew I reciprocated every bit of it that I'd sent him off to his doom without a chance to tell him… well, anything of value.

Dramatic, maybe, but I had clarity for the smaller issue, and I could only repair things with him when we were together again. And we *would* be together again.

I fired off a response telling József I'd try to connect with him soon and then slipped into the meeting with the other embassy staff who had a hand in this event. As the lead, I'd been in touch with everyone via e-mail, but it was great to see them face-to-face and know we were just twenty-four hours from executing everything we'd been working on for months.

By noon, we'd dispersed, and I was on my way to the hotel. I'd never met the women speaking at the symposium, and only one of them had agreed to meet for lunch, but I couldn't trick myself into forgetting I was nervous.

Juliet Christensen was an advocate for women and children the world over, and she put her money and her time where her mouth was. To meet this person who showed up everywhere from A-list Hollywood movie premieres and the annual Met Gala in cutting edge designer clothes to towns and villages torn by war in muddied utility pants and sweat-soaked T-shirts was kind of a dream come true. She'd agreed to come speak at the event on her experiences in Eastern Europe and what she'd learned about trafficking pipelines as well as a separate small session on women in nonprofit leadership.

Basically, she was a badass and I couldn't wait to meet her and get a feel for her. When I walked into the opulent lobby of her hotel, I instantly spotted her shaking hands with someone not far from the elevators. It was a gentle shake, and there was something familiar to it.

I approached slowly to give her time to finish the interaction. A cooler head than mine probably would've avoided looking at her entirely—but not me. Because if I was a fangirl of anything, it was powerful women using their power to do good things.

And maybe Ryan West, but that was beside the point.

Oh, look! I made it until noon without thinking of him once!

Okay, fact check reveals I'd already thought of him several times today, so this was a false victory. Our last moments together had left me burning with frustration with him and myself, so this time apart was probably well-timed. We needed to take a breath, and I needed to figure out how I would handle him being gone. If one of my major concerns about being with a soldier was the time apart and knowing he was in danger, then this was a necessary hurdle for me to jump... or trip on.

And in truth, the disagreement or argument or whatever we were going to call it had reminded me that what I'd never wanted was to partner with someone who was going to treat me like a subordinate. I'd seen relationships where that dynamic was one of a sergeant major and a soldier, not a husband and wife. Though I'd witnessed such an awful dynamic with civilian friends, too, and I'd also seen many loving, equal partnerships amongst my friends and their soldier spouses.

So really, I'd pushed back against an idea, again, and not the man I knew and felt so much for. I'd pushed against the prospect of a soldier and an alpha male bossing me around instead of slowing my frustration and acknowledging how Ryan wanted me safe, yes, but he did respect me to make my own choices. He was never going to be someone who didn't tell me what he thought, and he was going to do it with confidence, but it wouldn't be to control me. It was because he cared.

"I'll see you again soon, honey. Have a good meeting." The blond man winked at her, then sauntered off, and only then did I see a guy in an all-black suit press the elevator button for him.

Juliet turned toward me and stutter-stepped. "Emily Wender?"

A surprised laugh tripped out of me. "Yes. Wow, I can't believe you recognized me."

She held out a hand. "Of course I do. I'm so pleased to meet you in person."

Her warm, firm handshake proved just how classy and polished she was. Or maybe I was just freaking out meeting this extraordinary person whose organization had won every possible humanitarian award and I wouldn't be surprised to see her on the Nobel Peace Prize short list someday. She was one of four amazing women speaking, and I couldn't tamp down the rising excitement.

"Forgive me, but do I know your friend?" the blond Adonis with security butted in with a charming smile and a hand on Juliet's shoulder.

Juliet smiled, completely at ease. "Simon Bellingham, meet Emily Wender. She's the woman in charge of the symposium. Emily, Simon is an old friend, but you may also know him as the CEO of Synergies Corporation."

My stomach lurched with nerves as I extended my hand to the familiar person. Once she mentioned his name, I instantly recognized him. He was the type of man who sailed on yachts around the world and whose company did things so far above my understanding, I didn't actually know anything about him other than that he was one of the types of rich businessmen whose net worth started with *b* and I was pretty sure he popped up in entertainment mags with gorgeous actresses and models on his arm here and there.

"Nice to meet you. Are you in town on business?" I asked like a fool, as though any answer he could give would make sense to me.

He gave me a beaming white smile. It was honestly stunning. He had a manicured look about him, but there was something in his energy that was friendly and disarming... until I remembered he was one of the richest men in the world, and that made me feel a bit odd shaking his warm hand.

"The pleasure is mine, Emily. Juliet mentioned she'd be here, and I could see her for a few hours if I managed to get here to catch my elusively busy friend. I've got a quick teleconference, but best of luck with the symposium. See you soon, Jules," he said, directing this last thought to Juliet, who gave him a soft smile.

The elevator scrolled open as though he'd commanded it, and his bodyguard followed him in. He'd moved to looking at his phone but gave us one last charming smile before the doors closed.

I was still blinking, still wondering at the odd way my heart had accelerated in this stranger's presence. Was I awestruck simply because he was wealthy? I didn't like what that said about me.

"He has that effect on people," Juliet said with a small, breathy laugh.

My gaze switched to her. "I'm not even sure why I'm flustered. I am happily in a relationship. I'm not particularly interested in money. I hardly ever find blond guys attractive, but…"

It wasn't a reaction like I had with West. It wasn't that kind of physical interest and longing and *click*. But it was an oddly heart-racing response, and I wasn't sure I liked that it was happening at all.

Her grin widened. "There is genuinely something about him. I don't feel it anymore, but years ago when I first met him, I was the same."

I eyed her discreetly as we moved toward the hotel restaurant where we'd planned to dine. "Are you… together?"

She coughed delicately. "Uh, no. Just good friends for years now. His company and my father's partnered on a project years ago, and I've known him ever since."

Ah, the ways of the billionaires. For a second, I'd forgotten that Juliet Christensen came from *the* Christensens. They were a Scandinavian-American family who'd made their fortune in the tech boom of the late eighties and nineties, and then the fortune kept going. Again, I had little understanding of their world, and I was fine with that.

What Juliet Christensen did with her time and money, especially considering she didn't have to work a day in her life, made her good people in my opinion.

"Shall we?" she asked, a hand out suggesting I lead the way into the bustling restaurant.

"We shall." And so we went and settled in for a lovely meal and even better company.

By the end of the afternoon, I'd spent a little too much

time with Juliet, a woman I now considered a friend, and an achy sensation filled with longing had wormed its way into my heart. I wished I could call West and tell him about all of this, but we weren't in contact while he was on his mission. I'd sent him a few texts he'd see when he got back to the States, and other than that, I'd sent him an e-mail with my trip details because it'd felt weird not to. I doubted he'd see them, but I'd never actually talked about the trip specifics in terms of dates and times for the event and I wanted him to know.

I wanted him to know everything about me, even these small things like how much I liked Juliet and how down to earth she was. I wanted to tell him about how she'd insisted we order dessert and then pulled me in for a genuinely warm hug before we parted ways.

I couldn't wait to see the event inspire the women of Budapest and the surrounding areas, and then I couldn't wait to get back home and see Ryan again.

CHAPTER TWENTY-ONE

West

I gritted my teeth as South stomped around the safe house an hour from Budapest and ranted about the mess we were in.

"What is the point of hauling apples out here, blowing out of town like we've got a job to do, and then showing up to find out the intel is wrong? And not only wrong, but so f-fudge brownied up the à la mode that we've spent valuable time and resources and all we've gotten is jack *chips*."

North's eyes were closed, and he'd gone to his Zen place somewhere in his mind, but slowly, the calm had been stripped away, one non-swear word at a time. When South tossed a pile of papers into a burn bag and grumbled his way out of the room while East continued typing furiously on his secure laptop, one of North's eyes opened, then the other.

"He's unusually cranky."

I sighed out some of my own frustration. "I can't blame him."

North ran a hand through his hair. "I can't either. I feel the same way. I just don't put it quite so... colorfully."

East's eyes ticked up to meet mine, then returned to his work. That was as close to a "same" as we'd get from him while he was focused.

I stood to stretch and patted North on the back. "He's making an effort. I'm not going to criticize that."

North stood, too, and we moved to fill coffee mugs. We didn't always end up with coffee makers in our secured rooms, but this last week had been one disappointment and trip back to the literal drawing board after another. We'd been chasing our tails trying to find out who was still leaking intel from the embassy and, more importantly, where it was going. We'd flown out and executed a sting operation at a warehouse outside the city based on intelligence we'd received from a Kappa Sector contact, but by the time we'd shown up, the place was abandoned.

Add to this the fact that in the week we'd been here, two more women had been taken from government staff, and we were going crazy. It was as though everything we'd done two months ago had been useless. If we'd gotten the mole and taken out the supply chain, why was all this still happening?

Clearly, there was a secondary source, or someone had moved in on the former operation and was trying to get it running again. This could happen—sometimes, it felt like playing whack-a-mole when you took out minor players, because three more would spring up in the same place. We were missing something, and we were determined not to leave here without discovering what.

"Froot loops and alphabet soups, that's annoying."

South's voice came from down the hallway, and North and I exchanged an amused look.

South's kid-safe expletives were proof he was spending time with Naomi and the boys and he was bound and determined to stop swearing. When we asked him about it a while back, he'd shrugged and said, "I want to be a positive influence on them."

And so, when he let off steam, we no longer heard the barrage of Bostonian-accented profanity we used to. Now we got colorful combinations of food-related expletives.

While North savored his coffee, I slipped into a chair and decided to sign into my email. I hadn't had time since we'd left and I didn't expect to have anything time-sensitive, but I needed a minute to do something with my restless energy. I'd worked out and showered before our virtual teleconference with Commander Patch, and after the thorough reaming we'd received, I needed to think about something else. Jimmy and the rest of the squadron had headquartered at a larger setup an hour or so from here, and we were all recuperating after the miserable failure. We weren't used to failing, frankly, and when it happened, we felt the blow keenly.

Maybe I'd send an email to Emily.

Okay, fine. I was signing on to see if there was anything from her.

I didn't like the way we'd left things, and I wanted some sign of how she was feeling about it. If there was nothing, it was safe to say we were in more trouble than I'd realized. I was never going to be the kind of man who saw danger near someone I cared for and didn't do something about it. That went against the very fabric of my being. But I couldn't fault her for feeling a little smothered by my forceful suggestions. I'd need to work on how I presented things like that to her.

South wandered back in with a bowl of something that looked like oatmeal, chewing aggressively. The man was a bottomless pit and hadn't eaten nearly enough, so at least he'd calmed down enough to get some food.

"Here's my thing. Who's leaking?" He took a giant bite of oatmeal, chewed, swallowed, and continued. "We got Gordon and he went down easy. I didn't get the uh-oh feeling about anyone else we talked to, and we've been over it a hundred times. Now we've got two more women missing and some jackfruit laughing all the way to his foreign bank account that we can't trace."

East still hammered away at his keyboard while I waited for the last security check of my computer before it loaded my email. My heart rate had ticked up in anticipation, but I tried to keep my mind tuned into the conversation.

"Maybe it's not anyone at the embassy. Maybe it's someone embassy adjacent. We've checked out all obvious staff, service personnel, everyone. Kappa's guidance was sound in terms of location, but someone got there first. From what they and State have told us, Volkov's still on his heels. Finding the cache and taking out the supply chain did make a difference to him, so if someone's still feeding intel, it's not to Volkov's people." North leaned back in a chair, head cradled in his hands as he eyed the ceiling. "So what if it's someone between... someone we aren't seeing."

His logic was good. Maybe we'd gotten the wrong guy, or maybe we'd gotten *one* of them and the other was outside the scope of where we'd been searching.

East snapped, one crisp *click* of his fingers signaling he'd had an idea. His typing grew even more furious, the furrow of concentration in his brow deepening, and we all watched because ninety-nine percent of the time, it meant he'd figured out something that would break open the whole problem.

"Thank Parker House rolls, he's onto something." South slumped into a chair and gobbled the rest of his oatmeal.

My heart leapt as my screen loaded, and I saw not one but *two* emails from Em.

"What was the name of the guy sniffing around Emily?" North asked.

I glanced up. "József Mólnar."

Like I'd forget, especially after he'd been the catalyst that had started our disagreement. It shouldn't bother me, and I'd tamped down the idiotic jealous reaction which had done me *no* favors in that conversation, but I wished she'd been willing to hear me out about him.

Well, she had. And I had to trust that she'd do what she thought was best even though I hoped she'd do what *I* thought was best and just blow the guy off with a "best of luck in life, pal" farewell text.

"He's a friend of an embassy local. State cleared him," South added. North was now situated behind East, watching his screen.

The lure of Emily's words drew my focus back to my own screen. She'd moved into my place, which gave me a burst of satisfaction and something like anticipation, too. She wouldn't have done that if she were upset, at least very, after our disagreement. She'd told me about having brunch with her friend Katie, whom she hoped I would meet some-time, and Rob apparently stopped by once a day whenever he was on the compound. Good man.

I itched to respond so she'd have something from me but opened the second email right as North sucked in a breath so loudly, it halted my progress.

"What?" South asked right as East worked his magic

and sent a photo up to the display monitors so we could all see.

"József, got it," South said, impatient.

He has no idea.

"He had a dual-layer and I just cracked it. Actual name is József Farkas. I'm sorry I didn't catch it before."

East's demeanor had become what could only be called thunderous, no doubt in frustration with himself for missing what he was now showing us was József's fake identity that we'd originally seen and the layer under it... the one we'd thought we'd uncovered and the reason I'd wanted her to be cautious.

Then he clicked and scrolled, revealing the man's true identity.

"Shortcake."

The rest of our statements were less sweet but all meant the same thing. József wasn't a simple foreign national threat. He was a deeply embedded part of Maxim Volkov's organization—or he had been. He was what we'd call a captain, a mini-boss, and he'd been right in front of us the whole time.

"No. State cleared him." Of all of us, South hated missing things most, though none of us would take this lightly.

"It fits. He's deeper in than we thought, and we didn't connect him to Volkov, only to the potential for insidious action. I have a feeling he's not still working for Volkov, though... I'm guessing he's thinking bigger. He saw his chance and we handed it to him on a silver platter—took out a scapegoat, got him off the radar, crippled Volkov, and opened the door for more opportunities." North paced the room with anxious energy.

"And everything Emily told you absolved him even

more—he'd never pushed her for information, never made overtures. How he made it past State's checks as a friend of an LES at the embassy—Damn, he got us." South had stood and started pacing, too, but for me, everything had slowed.

The air had stilled and an eerie sense of knowing hit. I'd felt it before and now, here it was again as my eyes dropped to Emily's second email.

Her trip.

To Budapest.

My heart stopped for a beat as I read her words.

The symposium is a two-day event. I'll be there early and hopefully have time to meet the speakers, plus I'll maybe stop by and see my landlady, and if I see József, I'll be sure to arrange for him to come to the event hotel. I don't think that'll seem weird, and then we'll have the security from the event and it's nice and public like we talked about. I hope that'll allay your fears. I want to make sure you know I do appreciate your wisdom and care for me. I hope you can respect my decision.

József.

This had to be connected. There was no way he was József Farkas and also happened to be a nice guy who was friendly to Emily under a different name. He wanted something from her, and it made no sense that he'd bother to keep in touch after she'd moved.

But he'd met me. And if he'd seen me with her and knew, even had an inkling about who we were, then she was in grave danger. If he made me, if he somehow had intel that put me in any kind of special operations unit rather than the DoD training cover we'd used while there, then of course he would be much more interested in Emily than he had been before.

And this also indicated just how far up he might be reaching, if he had access to such information.

She was in Budapest now. Today was the second day of the event she'd traveled for, and she planned to see the man who had not one but two hands in the smuggling of information and likely women from the US embassy to one of the worst criminal organizations in Eastern Europe—or, even better, he was trying to move his way up. And honestly, the most obvious choice would be for him to slip into the Talon Network directly instead of having Volkov as the middle man.

My blood chilled.

"What is it?" East asked.

My jaw locked tight, mind momentarily numbed out. His words hit me like a defibrillator, jarring me back to clarity.

"Emily's here. She's in danger."

And there was the fear I'd claimed I never felt when she'd asked just days ago. I gave myself a minute to feel it, the thundering heart and clawing feeling ripping into my gut, screaming that everything between us had been too good to be true. I embraced the terror of losing her, of finally finding someone I wanted more with and then losing her like this, let it wrap around me... and then I mentally crushed it in the name of doing what I knew we had to do. Whatever I had to do to get her back.

And after so long, so many missions together and life's ups and downs, they knew. They instantly sprang into action, loading weapons and contacting headquarters back home for all the permissions we'd need.

We had a break in the case. We knew the bad guy.

We just had to make sure we got to him before he got to Emily.

CHAPTER TWENTY-TWO

Emily

Juliet beamed at me as I marveled at her and the three other women.

"You're all incredible and I'm so grateful you set aside your time to participate in this. I hope it's been rewarding for you." I clasped my hands in front of my chest, so much joy and hope and positivity beaming out of me, I could hardly contain it.

"It's been wonderful, truly. Any time you plan something like this, put me on your list," Juliet said, and the other women added their agreement.

The highlight so far had been speaking to young women about opportunities in leadership and non-profit work. We'd created several internship opportunities in each of the organizations run by our esteemed guests as well as a basic overview of early opportunities within the State Department and other parts of the US government.

While this wouldn't apply to the young women from Hungary, there was a decent contingency from international high schools and even surrounding countries' US military and State Department-associated families.

I talked with the women for a few more minutes before they would head out to their final speaking portion. The served lunch and breakout sessions of the afternoon had been so wonderful, and I already had ideas of how to expand this project internationally and back in the US.

Frankly, I was buzzing and so, *so* happy. I went to the stage to announce the speakers, then slipped backstage so I could sneak back into the audience and enjoy the final moments of this conference.

Maybe it was the adrenaline or the general elation thrumming through me at a job well done, but when I saw József standing next to the stage exit door, I didn't stop and think, *That's odd. I told him I wouldn't have a chance to see him this trip.* I didn't think at all. I only tilted my head and whispered, "Hey! I didn't expect to—"

It was his gloved hand over my mouth that sent alarm bells through me, but I still felt that happy energy pulsing until his finger and thumb pinched my nostrils shut and my attempt to breathe in failed.

My eyes widened and my pulse shattered into a furious churn until it plummeted and everything went dark.

Piercing pain split into my brain like an axe into a stump. I eased my eyes open, and adrenaline crashed through me as I registered the dim lighting and dark, empty space around me. I'd been kidnapped.

József had taken me. He'd covered my mouth and nose and—

"You're awake."

The duct tape pressed against my mouth foiled my natural urge to gasp in response to hearing his voice and I sputtered, inhaling rough breaths through my nose to compensate as my body came back to itself. Hands tied behind me, seated in a chair, feet bound to the legs of the chair. Aside from the duct tape, it didn't feel like anything else was wrong other than my brutal headache.

Oh, and the bone-liquefying fear that coursed through me as the situation became clearer. This man I'd thought was a kind soul, a person I'd even begun thinking of as a friend of sorts, had abducted me.

Had he been behind the other kidnappings? The Cardinals had recovered the missing women and I'd assumed they'd apprehended whoever had been behind that, but maybe I misunderstood. Or perhaps this was all some really weird misunderstanding.

West had been right to be wary of József. So, so right. Wasn't his actual job rescuing people from kidnapping and dismantling terrorist organizations? Wouldn't he know? He did know, and I'd waffled just long enough to make clear I was here, in Budapest, and that József knew my schedule. Maybe I'd even made it all worse because I hadn't simply apologized for not being able to meet with him early on, but I'd felt bad. I'd grappled with the decision and ultimately felt like I shouldn't see him like West had suggested, but now...

West. My heart squeezed at the thought of him.

Where in the world was he? I wasn't sure, but I

wondered if maybe, he was nearby. Maybe he couldn't tell me, but he was somewhere close, working on figuring out what was happening. At the very least, when I didn't come home in a few days, maybe he'd notice.

Work would notice, too. And Naomi. And maybe even Lucinda, if I didn't check in before leaving again, though maybe not. It would seem strange if I wasn't there to thank the speakers again or emcee the close out of the conference, but not necessarily alarming.

"You've probably got questions, don't you?" József's voice got closer, but he was still behind me.

I squirmed a bit, but whatever material bound me to the chair bit into my skin, and though I considered myself a decently capable and tough woman, I wasn't about to muscle out of these restraints.

József stepped into view and looked down at me with such a fond grin, it sent a chill through me. Even now, he looked handsome and friendly. His blond hair was styled neatly, his spectacles featuring silver wire frames that were entirely unremarkable but lightly flattering, and his clothes were also unmemorable. I'd always taken these things as part of the person I'd gotten to know—a slightly shy but friendly young Hungarian man who just happened to be at the same café as me.

I inwardly cringed. How had I fallen for it?

Maybe because he was vetted by the embassy, and that made you believe he was who he said he was.

"Oh, I know, I know. It's hard to face the reality that you're an oblivious American rube and that you're now going to end up living a very different life." His smirk was like a smear of oil.

Jerking in my seat, I could do nothing other than squirm

to show him my frustration. Well, and I did make some sounds of frustration, but they were unintelligible.

He pulled up a chair across from me and leaned on his knees.

"You know, I'm not sure I'm going to pass you off just yet. I'll send the others, but maybe I'd like to keep you for myself a while. After all those pitying looks when my dates ditched me..." He shook his head like he'd caught himself getting off track. "The bigger point is, your Captain America is back in the US, your idiot ambassador still has no idea the women disappearing from his staff *are* the leak when they lay their pretty heads down on my pillow and tell me things they think are harmless, and that every time one disappears, so does his hope of figuring out who's getting intel..."

He sighed with such pure pleasure, warning spiraled through me anew.

"It's going to be a real disappointment when your Ryan Jacobs realizes he's the only reason you're here."

My brows furrowed, asking the question my mouth could not.

"I make sure to... *connect* with as many women from the embassy as possible." He grinned as though he'd said something he was proud of. "Take my word for it—they love a shy Hungarian man dazzled by their American wit. I may not look like a honeypot, but to lonely foreigners looking for a nice, handsome *friend*?" He laughed and circled my chair. "And the fact that I'm known by the embassy, dear friends with locally employed staff, just made it easier."

I jerked, wishing I could spit in his face.

"But I wouldn't have had all that much interest in you since you weren't going to be a useful asset to me long term until I saw *him*." He rolled his eyes.

I waited, a sick feeling slithering through me.

"These American soldiers think they're invincible. It's disgusting. And maybe he'll learn a little lesson now that you've disappeared. As for me? I'm moving up in the world. And you're going to be a nice little present for my new employer. He might even want to use you for leverage with the Americans, who knows. It should be fun."

He wasn't playing. And he had no intention of sending me back. I didn't know how he'd done it, but that little speech made clear he'd had a direct hand in abducting the women, and he'd done it to cover his tracks.

I tried to scream, tried to make any kind of sound to end this madness, but it was all just a cacophony in my head. He watched, his eyes drooping with a sick satisfaction at my ineffectual attempts.

Whatever bit of hope I'd held that he'd let me go winked out when he grinned and stood up.

"Ah, pretty Emily. You can shred your vocal cords and claw at your cuffs until your nails break, but you're mine now. And once I pass you off, well, take my word for it"—that smirk again—"there'll be even less point in screaming."

CHAPTER TWENTY-THREE

West

We entered the hotel at sixteen hundred to find the ballroom empty and one of the breakout rooms swarming with embassy personnel. East had called it in after talking with headquarters and getting the go-ahead—our suspicion that Emily wasn't safe, and more so, that we might've found a missing link in the intel for this whole mess.

Any attempt to contact Emily had failed. Before we'd arrived, the staff at the hotel and our embassy contact confirmed the worst—she wasn't in the building.

After a quick rundown of the situation from the hotel manager, embassy security officer, and local police, I saw the CIA station agent slip in the side door.

"She was definitely taken out the back door on the south side. It's all blocked off. Security cameras were conveniently shifted away, but—"

"On it," East said from where he'd set up at a small table with his travel laptop and was speaking low into the comms in his ear, likely to the nerds stationed back at HQ with the other teams.

"Excuse me." A tall woman with long blond hair pulled into a tidy ponytail at the back of her head caught my eye as she spoke. "Could I speak with someone about Emily Wender? Are you all here to help find her?"

"Let's not get ahead of ourselves. Of course, we suspect there's been an issue, but Miss Wender might've simply gone for a walk around the city and left her phone. It's only been an hour since the event ended." One of the lower-level embassy personnel tried to manage the flurry of concern.

"I don't think she meant to leave," the woman said, then extended her hand to me. "Juliet Christensen. I was a speaker at the event and had planned to talk with Emily after. She'd even remarked on having a drink at my hotel later. I really don't—"

Juliet jostled as East shoved his monitor in my face. He'd found side street imagery of a small SUV leaving the hotel around the time we'd estimated she would've been taken. While South drove here from our safe house, we'd all been working furiously to gather information, and this was the last piece. Our team at HQ had dug it up, and sure enough, it looked quite out of place.

"Sorry, ma'am. We've got a lead and as you can imagine, this is time-sensitive," I said, nearly crawling out of my skin with the need to bolt to the vehicle.

East stepped away mumbling sorry, I thought, though it was always hard to tell what he was saying when he spoke under his breath and didn't look up from his computer. Juliet waved a hand like she truly wasn't fazed.

"Go, please, you—" She coughed. "Shane?"

East froze and glanced up, evidently seeing Juliet for the first time. For a man as tightly controlled as he was, the small jolt to his body told a story we'd have to dig into later. He didn't speak, only turned and moved toward the door, thawing the rest of us out.

We were moving, running as I dialed the number to update our command team back home. We'd alerted them to the discovery about József and our concern Emily might be at risk. It was time to let them know we were going in and, if we were lucky, we'd find Emily, the other women, and a lot more. We'd find the key to everything that'd gone wrong and we'd break this open wide.

Within minutes, we were on the road, South driving like a bat out of hell and the rest of us on task. North was working the intel East had gathered on possible trajectories for the car. He'd found traffic cameras out of the city, but after that, he'd lost the vehicle. In the next ten minutes, we'd need an update or we'd be sunk, at least from this angle. But now that we knew who, exactly, we were looking for, the path became clear.

East murmured into his comms unit with our team back at the mission HQ not far from our safe house. The secondary team would join us as soon as we had a confirmed location and with them would come close air support and more eyes in the sky.

This guy wasn't getting away, the women would be recovered, and we'd be one large step closer to shutting down another arm of Volkov's network if he was still a part of that. Even better, if he was striking out on his own, we'd shut him down entirely. And if we were truly lucky, we'd collect some crumbs on the Talon Network if he had any knowledge there.

"Got him."

East's hunch must've been right, and South followed the directions East gave as he sped into the Hungarian countryside.

I found my calm. It'd been just out of my grasp since I'd seen Em's email about being in Budapest. I was used to the adrenal response my body gave to ready me for battle, for a mission, for an op, but I was completely blindsided by the foggy quality my thoughts would take on when someone I cared about was at risk.

The Cards had all had moments of peril, no doubt, but this was different. Emily wasn't trained. She didn't know how to evade or escape. She didn't know how to be a captive, and though operators trained for how *not* to be taken, we were also trained on how to withstand torture and the psychological component of being a prisoner.

No way to pretend otherwise—Emily mattered to me. More than anyone had in a long time.

In truth, even though it seemed unusually fast, the calm that settled into me as the engine churned and carried us closer to her, the clearer I felt about the reality of my feelings for her.

Yes, it was soon, but it wasn't as though we'd just met. I had a lot more to learn about her, a lot more to experience with her, yet I wanted a future with her.

The acceptance of that realization anchored me in my seat and I exhaled slowly.

"You breathing normal yet?" North asked with a glance back at me.

"Not just yet, but getting there. I'll be normal when we've got Emily *and* the idiot who dared to take her."

The minutes flew as we coordinated with HQ and they got their drones in place so we had eyes on the buildings, and soon thereafter, a clear decent map of the area.

Normally, the Hungarian countryside wouldn't offer us much in the way of satellite availability and connection, but technology had come a long way, and there were some billionaires who liked to give gifts like the use of their satellites where the US had blank spaces.

We'd kitted up in our gear before we left our safe house, so we each wore black tactical gear from head to toe, with the best body armor anyone had to offer in thin slabs over our torsos. The regular army's body armor was incredibly heavy, and though ours had weight to it, EMU got the best gear in the world—and I'd take any advantage I could if it meant I'd be faster, quieter, better at getting to Emily.

We had small pouches and pockets full of an arsenal of weapons. We carried rifles, handguns, flash-bangs, knives, and any number of other tools and accessories to assist in whatever we might face. I hoped we'd need very few of them today, but we'd be ready for anything.

We could've breached the building, but risking a noisy entrance with explosives also brought on a larger possibility that any hostages could be injured. If we were right—and all the intel East and our secondary team en route to join us had gathered in the last few hours pointed to the fact that we were—then there were a small handful of women being held in this building.

The car from the security footage had pulled into one of the loading bays at the far end of the building, but the door had been left open. We'd left our vehicle a quarter mile out to prevent any motor noise from alerting them and jogged into the building area at a clip that left us just shy of breathless. The adrenaline helped, but so did our persistent training. I signaled for us to approach and we fanned out, moving swiftly and silently, weapons drawn, before collapsing into a single file as we slipped along the side of the car and arrived at a door.

Second in tight formation, North stepped out and lunged for the door, swiftly tugging it, and miraculously, it gave. If they were expecting company, they weren't doing a very good job of shoring up the exits.

That was great news because it meant they weren't expecting us and they wanted us to come on in—or so we had to assume, right? We didn't want to get cocky and assume they had zero awareness of our presence, but if they were leaving the veritable front door open, they must've felt pretty darn secure.

We filtered inside one after another, completely silent, moving with the alertness we brought to every second of a mission. Over a decade honing this dynamic, we hardly needed the hand and arm signals we used, but one rule we never broke was to make things clear and never assume. Sometimes, one of us had an insight and that might change what we expected him to do, so we had to watch, listen, and respond.

Down a dimly lit hallway and at the end, I checked the view and pulled back. I held up one finger to signal one man standing guard. Then we launched, no hesitation, and in seconds had subdued the man. In an effort to maintain our silence, we'd used hand-to-hand combat whenever possible. Also, we would potentially want to interrogate the people here. Most likely they knew nothing of use since, as we'd seen so far, very few of the underlings knew anything about the larger Volkov organization, and definitely not that it was even a part of the Talon Network. But we couldn't dismiss an opportunity to check.

Another hallway, another guard, and then we hit the jackpot. We attacked a group of three guards with as much momentum and swiftness as we could muster before they got shots off, and fortunately, none of them had anticipated our arrival.

Whimpering caught my attention as I slowly lowered one unconscious guard to the floor, and I turned right as North and East rushed into the room, weapons raised. Three women screamed as best they could behind the gags in their mouths and scrambled to the side of their cage.

Yes. Their cage.

A familiar sense of darkness sent a shiver throughout me. I had seen the worst of human depravity and this was one of them. Caging a person, selling them, acting like anyone can own another human being… it chilled me in a place that often took a long time to thaw out.

"You're okay. You're okay now. We're going to get you out," North said, pulling out wire clippers and addressing the locks.

"We're American soldiers. We're here to help you. We'll get you out as soon as we can." East's words came out low, solemn, and steady.

Two of the women nodded rapidly as though this would encourage them to do any more while the other one just shut her eyes and shuddered in the corner.

"We've got this. Find Emily." North got the cage open and reached out a hand. The two women who were responsive reached for him and shuffled out as though their bodies were aching.

"Incoming in four."

The voice came over the radio signaling our other team would be here soon. Too long to wait in case anyone was tracking we'd entered the building, but soon enough, we'd overtake the scene and no one would be sneaking away tonight.

East coaxed the other woman out with low, gentle words. Sometimes, it surprised me how he'd speak in these circumstances—to women, to children, to people taken hostage or horrified by whatever they'd just lived through. But it wasn't that he was without compassion. Sometimes, I wondered if he tended toward silence because he felt so deeply, he lost words for it.

Once South and I had pulled the passed-out guards' bodies inside the room, we stood watch at the entrance to this space. No one came down the hallway or attempted to enter. After a few minutes, one of the women spoke.

"They've been busy. Something changed." Her voice was rough but clear.

"Any idea what?" North asked.

"No, but they seemed happy or something. No idea why," she said, looking at us like we'd know.

That was enough for me. "North and East will stay with you for a minute. South and I are going exploring."

South gave me the nod and we moved, quick and quiet, leaving our teammates to tend to the women. Hopefully, within a matter of minutes, we'd have backup from the other EMU team and these women would be on their way to get medical attention.

We moved at a clip just above a jog. We'd entered on the south side of the building, but we'd found the women halfway around since intel had told us there was a critical mass of bodies here based on heat signatures.

I internally calmed the jittering voice that said even if we found Emily unharmed, this would be something she'd have to work through. An event like this in a person's life could strip away the sense of security we all carried around until it was violated.

I'd make sure József and anyone else involved would pay for stealing this from these women, and from her.

"We've got a squirter heading northeast to building four-two. Raven two's got visual."

The update came over comms from our air support surveillance. Since we'd been working on a raid the last few days, we had all the resources in place and now they were in action. The ravens were our drones, and they'd keep eyes on whoever ran out of the building.

South and I both halted abruptly when we saw light shining under a set of double doors.

I made eye contact with South for a second, the moment holding like it always did before a major action, and then we breached the door, weapons raised, and moved.

There could be no hesitation. There could never be a moment where we faltered. This didn't mean we went in guns blazing. We were trained to see, evaluate, and then shoot, and to do that all in fractions of seconds when full seconds would mean death to our targets or ourselves.

The horror of the moment stretched out like I saw it through tempered glass, blurry and slow, until my brain snapped in. The buffoon guarding Emily saw us and moved from where he'd been talking on a phone to crouching behind Emily, who sat bound to a chair, and jammed the muzzle of a gun to her temple.

He cowered behind her, her eyes wide, watching as we kept coming, and South took the shot, a familiar muted *crack* and *thunk* sounding as we went. We didn't stop as his body dropped away, and Emily started shaking. South had his weapon at the ready while I cut the restraints, then gently peeled away the tape as best I could.

She reached for me before I could say anything.

"Thank you. Thank you for coming for me."

I hugged her to me with one hand as I slipped the knife into its sheath on my vest. My kit made me bulky, and I wished I could feel her body with mine, but the strong grip of her arms reassured me as well as anything could've.

"I'll always come for you." I kissed her head. "Thanks for being patient. I'm sorry we're late." I pulled back and soaked in the disbelieving shake of her head.

"What time is it? How long have you been looking?"

The sound of footsteps and voices interrupted us, and I eased her away from me as she tensed, so I took her hands in my gloved ones. "These are our guys. You're safe. I need to go get our pal Joe and have a chat with him."

She exhaled sharply and nodded. "Go get him."

And that was it. No clinging or begging or crying, any of which would've been completely understandable. Instead, she just sent me to do my job and get the bad guy.

Right.

If I hadn't already realized how deep my feelings ran, that would've clinched it. I loved her toughness, yes, but I also loved that she got it. She understood the job—that the mission came first. This would be the only time *she* was ever the mission, no doubt, and now the second part—apprehend József and find out exactly what he knew.

Leaving Em in the care of capable hands, I jogged to catch up with East as air support updated in my ear.

"He's in the building, likely right inside the south entrance. Ready for call out?"

The commander, who was located at our headquarters miles from here, gave the order. "Call him out. Let's see what happens."

Raven Two dropped low, and a voice came from the speaker inside it. "József Farkas, exit the building. You are surrounded. If you choose not to exit, we will enter and retrieve you."

I chuckled at the word choice. There was a common script, but Kellen, our drone guy, loved to mix things up when he knew the people spoke fluent English. It wasn't his best idea, but the message was clear. He repeated it, and still no Joe.

"Bangers," the commander ordered, and that was the call for me and the other EMU operators currently tucked behind walls and even a large truck parked between the warehouse where we'd been and the building where Joe had hunkered down to step in.

I moved as East, Dex, and Frank did, too. They slipped in line behind me and we skimmed the wall, then stopped at the doors. East nudged it wide with a boot, and I tossed a primed flash-bang. In seconds, the fuse hit and the explosions sounded, bright flashes and bangs that would feel to József like they were coming from all angles.

He was lucky he'd made it out of the warehouse alive, and if he happened to have prepared for the flash-bang, he wouldn't make it out of here. I'd long since made peace with death and the tolls of war, but I wanted him to play the game. I *needed* to hand him over to our operator interrogators, and I wanted them to learn everything possible about Volkov's organization and, ideally, the Talon Network.

In seconds, we were moving, slipping in the doors and checking every corner of the empty room. I walked directly to the man in a crouch with his hands over his head. Before he'd even lifted his head, I grabbed his arm and tucked it behind his back. There was no point speaking yet—his ears would still be ringing from the explosions, and he might not yet be clear of the adrenaline spike and disorientation that tended to come along with bangers.

I marched him, both hands behind his back, legs stumbling, toward the armored vehicle waiting to move him, East keeping his weapon trained on him in case he got any fun ideas. Dex and Frank opened the doors and radio chatter melted off as we confirmed we had him, he was in custody, and we'd be moving him to the HQ before he had a chance to see any of the women he'd abducted. When I shoved him into the back of the truck, he turned around and spat at me.

"You think this matters?" he shrieked.

I didn't respond because why would I? It did matter. We'd recovered four abducted women and he would never hurt anyone again. Whether it led to anything more didn't make or break the success of this mission. Anything else was bonus.

"Someday, he's going to kill you all," he said, a vicious edge to his voice.

"Who's *he*? If you want to go ahead and tell us who you're working for—"

"I'll never tell you anything. I don't even *know* anything to tell. That's why he's so brilliant," he snapped back.

Likely because whoever he was working for now, there was a higher level of compartmentalization.

"Maybe you really don't know anything. That's a shame. Though if it's who I suspect, I can say it is quite likely you will die at his hand," I said, because he'd taken my woman and I was feeling a little irritable.

He sneered. "You'll get nothing from me. He'll come for me and you'll get nothing."

I leaned in and leveled him with a smile. "That's precious. He'd have to find you to come get you, and bad news, bud. You're officially a missing person."

I made an exaggerated frowny face and stepped back. East would stay and assist them to wrap this up so I could go. Dex and Frank gave me looks like they'd be reminding me of this rousing speech when we were all back stateside, then moved to secure the criminal while I went for Emily.

My woman.

I didn't know if she thought of herself that way—likely not. I didn't need to share this possessive thought with her considering our last full conversation, but I wouldn't stop myself from thinking it. Not until she made clear she didn't want that from me.

I had more clarity than ever now, and it was this: No one would hurt her again, and I wasn't going to waste another second pretending I didn't feel something for her.

CHAPTER TWENTY-FOUR

Emily

Exhaustion set in about ten minutes later as the adrenaline had worn off. It ebbed so quickly, I felt drowsy, or maybe that was the drugging effect of safety after literal mortal peril.

How did West do this all the time? I couldn't fathom the amount of training that went into not only staying calm and focused and actually rescuing people but coming down after it and not wanting to pass out for days.

Loud pops and bangs sounded in the air, and I must've startled so visibly that one of the guys set a hand on my shoulder.

"You're okay, Wender. Those are just bangers. Westy's getting the bad guy to give up the goat. He and East'll get the job done with the rest of the other team." South slipped an arm around me and gave me a little side hug. "You okay?"

I swallowed, wishing West were here. I wanted the comfort of *him*, of that familiar, and yet I'd take anything short of being tied up again, I supposed. Still, I was glad at least South was here, and I'd seen North checking on the other women they'd recovered. "Uh, think so. Are you? I mean..." I hesitated before saying it. "You shot someone."

His smile was kind and small. "I'm okay."

"It's just... I've never..." I didn't glance at the place where the man's body had fallen. I didn't think about how many inches had separated me from him or me from death.

"It's not something civilians deal with. But in a hostage situation, our mission is to get the hostage out safe. That's it. We're not going to try to reason with someone who has a gun pressed to your head. So they lose."

Air gusted out of me. "Literally."

He took my shoulders in his hands. "Yeah, literally. They lose because too many times if they don't, the hostage does. And that's not my mission. I don't need to know why this guy has you. What I know is he took you, and he's wrong for doing that and he already had his chance for a change of heart—every second leading up to when we show up."

I nodded, throat tight.

He ducked his head until he caught my gaze with his.

"Listen, right now might not be the time to say it, but this is it—" He gestured to the room full of EMU personnel and three women who must've been held in a different part of the building. In the distance, I thought I could hear a truck engine starting up. "This is our lives. It varies, but this is the kind of thing we do. If knowing what you do now, if seeing it and being a part of it firsthand means you can't be with West, then you tell him. Right away."

I swallowed, shocked into continuing my silence. He'd

pointed to the very thing I was so afraid of, but nothing about this made me want West any *less*.

It only made me want him—*love* him—more. To see him literally saving lives... it was amazing. And yes, it was terrifying to think of, but it wasn't something that was going to scare me away from him. It was in his fabric, that protector, hero, amazing man. What kind of woman was I if I couldn't love all of him, every bit of what made him the man I'd fallen for, even if it scared me?

I'd just witnessed the worst of what someone with truly evil intentions did when they wanted to control someone. It was a wildly unnecessary comparison, but Ryan's goodness and honor and care for me stood out in stark relief against what so many men in the world did to women. He would win in any comparison, though, not just against people who committed horrifying acts of enslavement, because he constantly chose to help. To rescue.

Maybe it was eye-roll-worthy, but... to be a hero.

It might be terrifying to realize, but witnessing him here, doing something so few people could do, let alone *would*... I was proud of him. Proud to know him and to call him mine.

"Dude, what did you just say to her?" North asked, knocking into South's giant shoulder.

South shot him a glare. "Like I'd tell you, you peanut butter cup."

North blinked. "Is that an insult? Or... a compliment?"

South's glare darkened. Both of these men struck me as generally sunny, so the juxtaposition was a bit startling. Though maybe my thinking was skewed since I'd just seen South drop a man with a single bullet from however many feet away.

North snapped. "Stating a fact, I guess? I do love me some Reese's."

South's lids dropped low over his eyes, and then he palmed North's face and shoved it back.

Their antics made me laugh, and that brief release gave me hope I'd recover. Not just from the adrenaline crash, but from all of it.

They were my friends. They could help me, tell me what to do. Maybe Ryan could help, too.

My heart squeezed and worry hit right as the man himself walked through the door. He had a foreboding edge to him when he was all dressed up in his body armor and helmet, rifle slung across his chest and pistol at his hip. Our eyes locked and he moved toward me, ignoring one of the men who started to approach him and only stopping when we were toe to toe.

His hands came up and cupped my cheeks, the grip of his gloves rough against my face. "You okay?"

Emotion hit, but I clamped down on it, not wanting to cry now after keeping it together this long. "I will be. Yes."

He nodded and stepped closer, then dipped his head low and pressed his forehead to mine—or really, the edge of his helmet, but that as as close as we could get with all his gear. "Yes. You will be."

His confidence in me, his presence here, it all confirmed the statement. I would be okay, at least in time. And *we* would, too—we'd be better than I could've ever imagined.

What felt like hours later but may have genuinely only been minutes, because time had turned into something unfathomable, we were finally wrapping up. I talked to the other women, who shared their terrifying experiences and further cemented selfish gratitude that my own version of the story had been mercifully brief. I watched the Cardinals interact with the women and the other EMU team as they cleared the building, and I caught sight of the vehicle where they'd put József trundling off with what I assumed was a group of EMU soldiers.

"Will they kill him?" I asked West when he noticed me watching.

"No. Not unless he does something stupid. Right now, he's cooperating. We gave him a choice to work with us or do things the hard way and he made the right choice. They'll get what they can from him and decide from there, but they're not going to just put a bullet in him. He'll end up in prison or he might end up back in the world. All depends."

I wondered what it depended on, but my mind was too muddled to focus on guessing. I nodded, oddly relieved to hear József's fate despite what he'd done. I wanted him punished, but I hadn't reached a point where having people killed was part of a day's work. Then West was ushering me forward with a hand on my back, easing my step into a large vehicle, and though I'd never asked, I assumed we were heading back to Budapest.

No sooner had they turned on the engine than I slumped in my seat and woke some time later as the door cranked open again.

"Oh my goodness, I'm so glad you're all alive." Juliet Christensen shoved past East and North, who'd opened the door, and she reached for me.

East scowled and started toward her as though he'd restrain her, but he stopped when she spoke again.

"Can I hug you? Are you okay? What a useless question. Oh, Amy, Sara, Joanne, I'm so glad you're okay, too."

She hugged me lightly, then reached for the women and pressed their hands together between hers. It was a warm, human gesture, something that would be comfortable and not intrusive.

Then my brain caught up, at least a bit. She'd worked with trafficked women and children before. She likely knew better than any of us how to handle the situation.

"You can't do this," East said, which struck me as very odd.

North shut the van door on his side and patted East's shoulder. "They're okay, man. Let's not—"

"She shouldn't be here. Why is she here?"

East's level of frustration was as unfamiliar to me as it seemed to be to North, whose brow had furrowed and his mouth had opened with no sound coming out.

"Shane, please." It was Juliet who responded. "I'm here because I care."

They locked eyes and just... stared. One beat, then two, East's jaw hard and Juliet's lips pressed into a thin line.

"Let's get you inside and we'll have the doc check you out," West said, gesturing to us to precede him into the embassy building.

I followed behind the other women, and West's hand settled low on my back again.

"I know where to go, you know," I said, trying for light-hearted instead of exhausted and shell-shocked.

He moved closer, slowing our pace. "Of course you do. I'm not touching you for your sake."

I swallowed and looked up at him. "Not that I mind, but why?"

He shook his head, his gaze flickering back and forth between my eyes. "For me. Because I'm reminding myself you're here and you'll be okay. That we made it in time."

I stopped completely and turned, throwing my arms around him again. I dipped my face into his, the skin of my cheek scratching against the rough Velcro collar halfway up his neck. "Thank you for coming."

His arms tightened around me. "Thank you for being okay."

A laugh gusted out of me. "Yeah, I'm pretty sure I didn't have a lot of say in that, which I'll definitely be talking to a therapist about at some point in the near future, but I'll take it." I pulled back and cupped his face with my still-aching hands. "I... I'm so glad it was you."

His gaze darkened. "Em, I—"

South's voice interrupted whatever West started to stay. "The doc says he really needs to get everyone seen soon in case he needs to transfer to the hospital. I told him Wender's doing okay, but he won't take my word for it."

I stiffened and released West and eased out of his arms, his hands sliding to grip my shoulders.

"What is it?" he asked, eyes flickering back and forth between mine.

"That phrase. *Take my word for it.* There's something..." Something just out of reach in my foggy mind that felt like, inch by inch, it was worming its way back in, trying to clarify and become something I could actually see. Trying to break through the exhaustion of the day.

"Not uncommon, but if it's ringing your bell, follow the lead. Have you heard it before?" West asked, and South stepped closer so he could hear.

I stared at the ground, willing my mind to clear. "Lucinda says it all the time, but it was—" With a gasp, I grabbed him. "József. He said it so weirdly, and it reminded me of Lucinda. It might not be anything but—"

"At this point in this mess, we're not going to ignore anything. Especially where József's first language isn't

English, it'd be a weird phraseology for him." He looked at South and the large man nodded and jogged off.

Hands still on my shoulders, he spoke with so much calm, I could hardly believe it in light of my racing heart.

"If you're okay for now, I've got some things to wrap up before I can call it a night."

West was so somber. None of that sparkling confidence or the hint of swagger. This was all focused, serious warrior at work. This was a man pursuing a lead that felt simultaneously unbelievable and obvious.

"Okay," I said, after realizing he expected a response.

"Can I come see you later? At your hotel?"

"Oh. Right. Sure," I said, less startled by his suggestion than the thought of going back to my hotel. Back to my suitcases and the explosion of travel-sized products in the ensuite bathroom and the touch of life before I'd been kidnapped by someone I'd thought was a decent person. Back to before I realized that my former colleague might just be responsible for selling government secrets.

He must've mistaken my response for discomfort with his idea. "If not, there's no pressure. I want you to—"

I gripped his hands to stop him. "I want you to come. I'd really like that. Please come to my hotel tonight."

A loud *clap* came from South. "Love to hear it, you two, now let's go see if Lulu is delulu."

West and I exchanged a look at this, but then he dipped his head and a mix of longing for him and relief that I'd see him later twisted through me.

"See you soon, Em," he said with a little nod.

"See you soon, Ry."

CHAPTER TWENTY-FIVE

West

We entered the same floor in the embassy where I'd seen Emily and Lucinda get off the elevator that night months ago now, but this time, I was wearing tactical gear instead of a tux. And this time, I had a feeling I wouldn't just be taking photos out of here.

We moved silently onto the floor from the stairs, not interested in the ding of the elevator alerting anyone to our presence. Light spilled from an office two doors down the hallway, and just inside, Lucinda Atterby stood with her back to the door, rifling through items on her desk and shoving them into a bag.

"Going somewhere?" I asked, weapon aimed at her from just outside the room.

She whipped around and startled backward into the desk. "What on earth? I'm just here collecting a few things after a long day at the hotel. Why are you pointing that thing at me like I'm some kind of criminal?"

I lowered it slightly but didn't put it away, because you never knew how things would go. "Unfortunately, I think you might be a criminal, Lucinda."

"What could possibly make you think I'd dignify that with a response? Take my word for it, you're going to regret these accusations when the ambassador hears about this."

There it was. *Take my word for it.* What a simple thing, and yet it'd tipped off Emily. Pride welled up in me, and no small bit of amazement that in the midst of a horrific day, she'd been able to connect the dots.

I clucked and shook my head. "I think not, Lucinda. And what you just said happens to be part of how we figured it all out—well, Emily did, actually."

"Emily. What does she have to do with all of this?" She sniffed, clutching her back with her computer to her chest.

"Well, she was kidnapped, as you very well know. And your friend József told us all about—"

"That little ingrate. I gave him everything he needed to get ahead and what does he do? He goes and takes the one girl I told him not to. I told him he needed to stop with that nonsense, that it was too obvious, and he—"

It was all we needed. I holstered my weapon and grabbed her arm so quickly, she dropped her bag. North caught it and set it aside, then took her other arm as East called it in.

"You just incriminated yourself pretty well there, Lucinda. Do you want to do any more monologuing? Maybe tell us about your grand designs or your altruistic reasoning for why you decided to betray your country? Don't tell me it was for money..." I chided.

"Of *course* it was for money! I'm paid a pittance and I

always have been. I've given my life to this country in its service and what will I have? A trail of patchwork virtual marriage counseling sessions in an attempt to save a marriage with a serial cheater and a job that will be filled the day I leave." Her eyes got misty.

"Aw, that sounds hard. Too bad treason is super illegal," South said so cheerily, I had to chuckle.

All the pieces were coming together, and finally, the wariness and sense that something was missing had come to a close. Next stop, we'd need to check in on Joe and see if apprehending Lucinda would loosen his lips at all.

József had just enough information to run the Budapest operation for Volkov's organization but nothing useful beyond the names and players locally and his one contact in the larger setup. When we'd dismantled the Volkov arm but hadn't caught him in it, he'd seen an opportunity to work for the authority himself rather than via Volkov.

Lucinda had, in fact, been the primary mole, and she'd set up George Gordon to take the fall for her when she found out he was selling information, just far less impactful intel. She'd apparently fed the names of the women József befriended to him and therefore had a direct hand in their abductions after they became wary of his pressing for more information. It was her suggestion for Gordon to go solo, likely so her gravy train didn't dry up when we took out the cache and the other guys in the organization, narrowly missing József's role.

"At least we found the girls and now that loop is closed."

North spoke into the silence of the car as we drove from where the other EMU team had taken József in Budapest. We'd been gone for hours, but I had updates from the doc that no one needed a trip to the hospital and the families of the three women we'd unexpectedly found had been contacted.

And Juliet Christensen had personally messaged me to say Emily was safely in her room now. I'd slipped her my number to do just that and to stay with Em if she wanted it, though I could see I wouldn't need to beg Juliet to be a friend to Emily.

"We should've caught him a week ago," North said, frustration lining his words.

East grunted. "We should've gotten all of this sewn up two months ago, the last time we were here. But when Kappa and State fed us bad intel, we didn't see it coming."

We could all hear the censure in his voice, but also recognized the accusation for someone not doing their job was aimed at himself—that he should've known the intel was bad, even though that was only possible with hindsight. There was no one harder on himself than East. I appreciated that he expected the best from himself and I could even acknowledge the value in assessing oneself.

That said, he wasn't the only one to blame. We'd all missed things.

Like the fact that Juliet and East clearly had history. This would have to wait... for now.

As team leader, I couldn't let him take it all on himself. "We all missed things, but we did what we came to do last time. We were waiting on more intel, and we thought we had good stuff from Kappa and CIA. They were wrong, too, and we can only do so much with faulty information."

His lack of a reply came as no surprise.

South heaved a huge sigh. "I'm over this grilled skirt steak. I want a break in this Talon Network braised beef bourguignonne so we can finally do something that actually solves a bigger problem."

"I'd say recovering trafficked women and rooting out the source of government intel leak counts for something," North said, a bit closer to the Pollyanna he tended to be.

"And I can't tell you how grateful I am we were already here for Emily." I would never stop marveling at the insanity or grace that allowed us to intervene and intercept her so quickly. I likely wouldn't ever let myself dwell on what would've happened otherwise.

South giggled. "Oh, sweet mother of all beef brisket with barbecue sauce, please tell me you're going to put a ring on it, Westy."

East grumbled, and North chuckled. "Someone get this man some beef before his expletives turn into four-course meals."

We all laughed at that, the tension and awareness from the day leaking out of us bit by bit.

"But seriously, it's happening, isn't it? I mean, she's it for you, I can tell."

South's words sent something hot and *right* through me. "It's a little soon to propose."

East's silence let me hear North's gasp and South's "Ha!" all the more clearly.

"I knew it!" South crowed.

"I'm so happy for you, man," North added, patting my shoulder from where he sat next to me in the back.

"We're just getting started. It's way too soon to talk about any of that, though," I said, the faint protest feeling odd on my tongue.

Hadn't I been thinking about how relieved I was that

she was okay, how much I cared for her and how my life would've changed if she hadn't been? Hadn't I been daydreaming of what it'd be like if she just didn't buy her own house and instead, stayed with me?

"Is it that soon? I mean, you've been dreaming about this woman for actual years, right? And real life, you've been dating well over a month. That's not all that fast for a military relationship, is it?" North asked, not so much razzing me as he was genuinely asking.

I might have dissembled and pretended not to know what he was talking about or downplayed the amount of time I'd been preoccupied with thoughts of her since that first encounter.

So instead of making it small, I simply said, "True."

South nodded in the driver's seat. "That's what I'm saying. And it's not like you just met back then. You spent a week together. You talked. You told *us* about her enough to make me think you were half in love with her, and I know you're direct. You would've scared her away if she hadn't been equally as interested in you when she ended up being on staff here."

Here. Budapest. An odd reunion, but I couldn't help but be grateful for it. *There are no coincidences.* Maybe that signaled we were meant to find each other, and when we missed the first time, we got a second chance, and then a third.

I hoped she'd feel the same considering all of this led to her kidnapping.

Would she blame me for what happened? Would she see this as an unredeemable side effect of being with me?

The guys dropped me at Emily's hotel, urging me to call them if I needed anything. I heard their unspoken meaning —if it turned out she didn't want me there. If she'd had a change of heart or the realities of what being with me meant. Not that abduction was to be expected, but even seeing the kinds of work we did. South had told me about their exchange about our work and it hadn't done much to buoy me.

Could I expect her to want me after all this? I didn't know. But it wouldn't be fair to make any long-term judgments off how she felt today anyway. She'd been through something traumatic, and if she needed time or space or anything I could give her, I'd do it.

A few minutes later, I'd navigated through the hotel to her room number and knocked gently. She didn't answer right away, and I'd already promised myself I'd only knock once more, then leave and try again tomorrow when she opened.

"Hey. Sorry it's later than I thought it'd be. If you don't want—"

Her arms came around me and pulled me close. I dropped my bag and crushed her to me. Damn, I couldn't remember when I'd been so relieved and desperate to see and touch someone.

"Come in," she said as she eased back from the embrace and stepped fully inside.

I followed and shut the door behind me, dropping my bag where I stood.

She turned, eyeing me. "Are you not staying?"

"I wasn't certain you'd want me to. There's no pressure."

I'd never felt so unsure in my adult life, but holding her and breathing in her soft, warm scent had shaken me. Or rather, maybe it was the fear I might never get to do so that had hounded me all day and I could take a full breath now that I was having the chance to be with her again. Either way, I was a different man than I'd been weeks ago. I was a different man than I'd been *days* ago. And I didn't know how to move forward.

But Emily seemed to. She padded toward me on socked feet and took my hand.

"Did you get her?" she asked, guiding me.

"We did."

"Good."

That simple. And at some point, she'd want the details I could share. But right now, after such a long day, I would follow wherever she led.

She walked us into the bedroom and turned to face me. I'd left my vest and weapons at our safe house with the Cards, so when she reached for the buttons of my uniform, nothing blocked her way. I watched as she unbuttoned the jacket and, after our gazes connected and I dipped my chin to confirm I consented, she pushed it back over my shoulders and it slid down my arms to the floor.

She reached for the cotton shirt tucked into my pants and tugged at the material until it came loose, then she guided it up and, as I raised my hands above my head, the shirt followed.

She released a shaky breath and her lashes fluttered. "You really are Captain America, aren't you?"

I laughed. "I am not a super soldier in that regard, no."

But her comment stabbed at the tension building, snapped it so it broke open and spilled out, filling every ounce of air in the room. I could no longer pretend I didn't need her, and thankfully, she was with me, as always.

Her hands clutched at my shoulders while mine crushed her to my chest, our mouths meeting in a desperate kind of reunion that made everything fade into the background. One of my hands sifted into her hair as I stepped closer, our bodies flush, and we kissed in a dizzying, devouring kind of connection that made me want to laugh and weep and claim this woman forever.

When she reached for my belt, anticipation thrummed through me, but reason crept back in, too. I stilled her hands and spoke against her lips. "Better let me do that. I'll get a shower and be out in a few."

If I'd expected her protest, I would've been wrong. She eased back and nodded, her gusty sigh sending a wash of warm breath over my bare chest and another crash of wanting through me.

I wanted Emily Wender in every possible way, but I also wanted us to have a conversation. If she'd pushed, I wouldn't have been able to resist her, but we were on the same page now. There would be time for more, I hoped, but right now, I needed a shower and sadly but wisely, I'd be taking it alone.

"I'll be out in a minute."

She nodded and let her eyes wander down over my chest, then gave me a fiery look and shake of her head. "See you soon."

CHAPTER TWENTY-SIX

Emily

As much as I wanted to let things go where our bodies clearly wanted them to, our minds had engaged and stopped us.

Stupid mind!

Actually, no. As I sat on the hotel bed and listened to the water turn off and made a valiant effort not to envision West and his stunning chest glistening with water and— nope, see, no. Because slowing down made sense. I'd had the weirdest day of my life to say the least, and I didn't love the idea of jumping into the next phase of my relationship with West as a way to seek comfort.

Honestly, I'd be seeking more than that. I wanted that closeness with him. I wanted to give him pleasure, and I'd very happily accept it from him, too. But body and mind at war, it was the heart that made me certain I needed to slow down.

We'd been through so much, and I hardly knew where to start—how to help him understand what I now knew. I'd never been more clear that I wanted him and his confidence and certainty, and that I knew very well I didn't need to fear him trying to control me.

West came out and inevitably, he wore only a towel pinched at his waist because the man might've saved me from being kidnapped, but he was now still on his mission to unalive me.

"Sorry. Clothes are out here." He notched his chin toward his bag as he moved to it and grabbed it with his free hand.

I sat back, hands behind my head, and grinned. "Oh, I'm not sorry."

He chuckled low and shook his head, sending heat throughout me yet again. How did he manage to make me feel so many things at once—heat and anticipation, relief and gratitude, longing and happiness.

"Be out in a sec," he said, then disappeared into the bathroom.

A few minutes later, he emerged in joggers and a bright white V-neck tee. He looked clean and masculine and comfortable and so achingly handsome.

"Come sit," I invited, patting the space next to me on the mattress.

He climbed on and settled in, leaning against the headboard and setting his hand between us, palm up. I took it and laced our fingers together, wondering where to start.

"I'm sorry for what happened," he said, and the gravity of his words, the sincerity there as though he'd had a hand in causing it, had me inspecting him.

"Why does it sound like you think you're to blame for it?"

"He wouldn't have bothered if he hadn't seen us together. He told you that himself, didn't he?"

I nodded, recalling how I'd rehashed everything I could remember from what he'd said to me to one of the female operators who'd taken my statement of what happened. Clearly, West had read it. "He claimed so, but that's not your fault."

"It is. I should've stayed away, but instead, I put you at greater risk. We underestimated him and that's on us." His jaw flexed with frustration. "But it's clear his interest in you increased because of our interactions, and when you came back, he saw his opening."

I squeezed his hand. "Sure, but that's not your fault. And it's not like I was telling you I didn't want you anywhere near me. Plus, didn't you tell me to avoid him? It'd only be fair if you said 'I told you so,' because you were absolutely right."

He shook his head, waving off the right to the justified victory. It wasn't about winning for him, though, and my heart squeezed with how serious he was.

"I could've lost you, and it would've been my fault."

Throat tight, I pressed a kiss to his lips. "You didn't. You saved me."

His silence was answer enough. He didn't agree that it wasn't on him, so I tried another tack. "Would it be fair to say the blame lies with József and his... boss or whatever that whole situation is? Not you?"

He grunted low. "Maybe. Still, though. I hate that you had to go through this." He turned, cupping my cheek. "I know it's too much and way too soon, but I care about you, Emily. I don't ever want to see you hurt or upset, and today..."

"Before you left, I felt like you were trying to control

me. And honestly, just saying this makes me cringe because I know that wasn't it, but in the moment, it just felt like I was boxed in. I was feeling so much for you and wanted to make you happy, but I was scared by that, and by how strongly you felt that you were right." I chuckled at the thought. "But I like that about you—I even like that we butt heads sometimes. I just... with you leaving and the stress of the symposium and not being ready to face how I felt, it went south." I urged his head toward mine and pressed a soft, slow kiss to his lips. "I care about you, too. And I'll never forget the relief I felt seeing you and South burst into the room like that. I will never forget how you saved me."

"I shouldn't have—"

I pressed a finger gently to his lips and caught his gaze with mine. "I can see we're going to work on this dynamic in our relationship."

"What dynamic?"

"The one where you accept that I'm right and you're wrong and that's okay."

He laughed, his smile a beautiful thing to behold, and then hauled me into his arms for a hug. His lips brushed my ear as he spoke. "I love you, Em. I hope that's not too—"

"I love you, too, Ryan West."

EPILOGUE

West

Summer was easily the worst season in North Carolina, but the camellias and azaleas were in bloom and the back yard looked fantastic. I'd been extra careful to keep them pruned and flourishing this year because they were setting the scene.

"Food's here, West," South said, hauling in a huge stack of cardboard boxes holding our catered food.

"Just lay it all out on the tables. People should be here any minute." I might've been a fool for the plan, but I was too far gone now.

I'd gotten all of Emily's favorite things—her favorite local Mexican food, her favorite guac, barbecue, favorite local beer, favorite people... I just hoped including everyone in this wasn't going to backfire royally.

North patted my shoulder and beamed. "Excited?"

I exhaled, feeling nerves snaking through me and wishing I was more calm. "Nervous."

"She'll say yes," East said with one hundred percent confidence.

Please God, let her say yes.

"Hey, we're here. How can we help?" Naomi wandered in with Danny and Benny in tow, carrying a cake container.

South moved to her like a magnet. "Is that your carrot cake? Did you make two?"

She gave him a confused look. "Two? No. I think someone else is bringing pie."

He grinned, his eyes all kinds of soft and sparkly at her. "Well, I feel bad no one else is going to get any carrot cake."

He lunged for the cake and she whipped it away, laughing and cheeks pinked. They were too adorable, but as far as I could tell, neither one of them had any plans to do anything about it.

"Thank you for bringing that. It's her favorite."

Emily had raved about Naomi's cake, so it was one more thing to complete the puzzle.

Jimmy arrived, as did a handful of operators I knew Em liked, including Rob Waverly. He moved to me, grabbing my hand and bringing me in close to pat my back in a hug.

"Congrats, man, this is awesome."

"Thanks. You guys heading out soon?" I asked, fairly certain it was his squadron's time to head overseas.

Thankfully, Volkov's organization hadn't grown another head, and with József out of the picture and Lucinda recently being convicted on multiple counts, things had been quiet on the Budapest front. Rob's team was heading out to deal with a different problem related to the growing issue the Talon Network presented. The Secretary of Defense had listed it as an organization of interest long before the intel we gained from both József and Lucinda, and it'd now become an official directive to uncover more about it.

"Yep, we roll out next week. Glad I could make it." He patted my back and then moved to help South set up the food on the tables.

Noah Miller and his hugely pregnant wife were right behind him.

"Thanks for including us, West. It's great to be here." Katie was so kind to come considering she was due any day now. They'd left their daughter at home since Noah's mom was in town, so they were looking at this as a night out.

I just hope it's not one that ends in me drowning my sorrows alone in my room.

In another fifteen minutes, everyone was settled in the back yard, music turned off, and I heard the doorbell. Everyone stayed quiet, bless them, and I shut the door leading to the back yard and moved to greet her out front.

"Hey, beautiful," I said, acting completely normal and not at all nervous.

"Well, hello to you," she said, hugging me and pressing a kiss to my cheek.

I'd planned to play up the evening as something normal for at least another minute, but I couldn't wait.

"Do you remember how you said I should've said 'I told you so,' about the whole mess in Budapest?" I asked, clasping her hand in mine and leading her into the living room.

"Yes. *Random.* Am I about to get a belated one now?"

She smiled as I stopped and turned toward her, taking her other hand in mind.

"I'm saying it now, but not for that. I'm saying it because I told you from the very beginning I could see something between us. I told you I was serious about us, that I wanted a future with you. And that I felt pretty sure you'd end up feeling the same way if you gave us a shot."

She swallowed hard and her face grew serious. "That's true. I remember all that."

"Well," I said, dropping to one knee and pulling out a small box. I flicked it open with my thumb and kept hold of her other hand. "I'd like to ask you to marry me, Emily Wender. You are strong and smart and funny and stubborn, and I love everything about you. Sometimes, it feels like we've lost a lot of time together, but I can't think that way anymore because I'm so grateful for the time we've had, and all I want is more of it. I know I'll mess up and I'll get too bossy or protective and you'll have to put me in my place, but I promise to love you and care for you and grow old with you, if you'll have me."

She'd been biting her lip, and a watery laugh came out. "Yes, I will marry you, Ryan West. And in this one instance, you can say I told you so."

Relief coursed through me—she said yes! I practically fist-pumped in victory and felt the oxygen flowing freely now that I could actually, fully breathe. *She said yes.*

I slipped the ring onto her finger and then rose to standing, pulling her into a kiss and hug. We were laughing and so full of joy, but I had one more little surprise up my sleeve.

"I hope you'll like this next part," I said, guiding her into the kitchen.

"Next part?"

"Trust me?" I asked and when she nodded, I put a hand over her eyes and guided her to the back yard door. We stepped out and walked a few feet before I moved my hand and everyone yelled, "SURPRISE!"

Emily laughed and covered her mouth before she turned to me and hugged me. I dipped my mouth to her ear.

"I wanted you to celebrate with your community. In just a few months, you've become indispensable, and not just to me. I wanted you to know how valued you are—how irreplaceable. And I wanted to bring all your favorite things to you, as much as I could."

"I love you, Ryan West. You're spoiling me."

I nuzzled her neck and kissed beneath her ear. "Not yet. But I plan to enjoy a private celebration of our engagement later, and then? Yes, I will."

Emily

I shivered with anticipation for the fulfillment of that promise and pulled him close to give him a quick, hot, passionate kiss in front of everyone before turning and accepting congratulations hugs from friends.

Katie and Noah gave me huge hugs and then excused themselves to have one last date night before their second baby came. I was honored they had shown up at all considering how brutally uncomfortable Katie looked.

Before she left, she said, "You're up next with this, you know that, right?"

Where before that might've made me roll my eyes or pretend like I didn't want the same thing, I wouldn't pretend now. I just shook my head and said, "Let me get married first, okay?"

So many congratulations and toasts, from coworkers who'd turned into friends in a matter of months, friends who'd begun to feel like family, and of course, my littlest friends.

Benny grinned and took my hand, jumping to be held, so I scooped him up. Danny looked at West, then back at me.

"Are you sure you want to marry him?"

Naomi coughed and nearly choked on her margarita. "Danny, that's rude."

"Oh, sorry. I was just asking."

I ruffled his hair. "I like that you're asking. And I like that I can say yes, definitely."

Truly, what a wonderful feeling. I'd wanted this for so long—this sense of belonging and also that knowledge that Ryan West was my person. We'd always had a connection, even before we'd spent any real time together, and seeing that grow and bloom over the last few months had been some of the best moments of my life.

"I can't blame you, girl. Well done." Naomi clinked her glass with one she handed me after I set Benny down, who'd seen South and yelled "Scotty!" and I was dropped like a hot coal.

"Thank you. But hey, I've been meaning to ask you, what happened about the mold?" They'd found mold in a storage closet last week, and she'd missed work today in order to be home for the testing after it looked like it extended down under the wood flooring.

She gave me a dire look. "It's bad. Like... we probably need to move out bad. They're coming next week to start remediation, and we're just going to stay out of the house as much as we can."

"What? No. You can't still stay there," South said, evidently overhearing her.

"Well, I'm not in a position to stay at a hotel until this is over," she said, her cheeks burning red.

"Of course you're not. You'll all stay with me."

My mouth dropped open and so did hers. But before she could speak, West hollered to get everyone's attention.

"Sorry to interrupt. I just wanted to say thank you all for coming and celebrating with us. We never imagined that an overseas mission could result in our reconnecting, let alone ending up here, ready to take the next steps toward life together." He circled an arm around me as I joined him at his side.

"I think you did imagine it, didn't you?" I asked, smiling up at him.

He ducked his head and lifted my chin with a light touch, and after kissing me softly said, "Oh, that's right. Told you so."

Everyone laughed, more than familiar with our teasing each other about things like this, and all I could say, from the bottom of my heart, was, "So glad you were right."

Thank you for reading West and Emily's story! Catch South in *Protected By South*, coming soon. If you haven't read Bri Williamson's story, don't miss it in Love Under-cover (you'll see all four Cardinals in there, too!) Stay up to date on all of Claire's new releases by signing up for her newsletter here.

AUTHOR'S NOTE AND ACKNOWLEDGMENTS

Thank you for reading Escaping With West. This book has been percolating for a while now and I'm so happy to have West and Emily's story down on the page. Thank you for reading and diving into a new sub-genre with me! I hope you enjoyed the Claire Cain version of romantic suspense.

Ironically, I used to joke I'd never write this kind of book—or I used to complain that this was all there was for military romance, which was why I started writing contemporary romance with military heroes. But as our lives have entwined with different parts of the military, this little unit has grown into existence to combine some real features of special operations in the military and some fun grabs from my favorite move franchise (*Mission Impossible*—IMF, EMU... see inspiration there?). It has been so fun to dive into this world and dream up heroes to match, so thanks for going along for the ride!

Thank you to my husband and family, and particularly my husband for answering questions about many military details. Any errors there are either due to creative license, or simply my error. I appreciate you suspending your disbelief enough to enjoy the books.

Thank you to Zee Monodee for sticking with me in yet another new sub genre. Thanks to Amanda Cuff for your quick proof, and thank you to Jamie McGillen for sneaking this one in during the realities of military life!

Thank you, as always, to my amazing beta readers

Amanda and Genny. This book had some issues and your feedback genuinely helped target and refine those from a reader standpoint. I'm indebted to you and hope we can get together IRL somehow this year!

Thank you to my Facebook group for being awesome and joyful and excited to read what I write. Thank you to the amazing Bookstagram community and ARC readers who so generously give their time to read and post about the books. Since I know not everyone will dive into this series, I'll just say thank you SO much for being here and supporting me through sharing about your reads!

And always last but never least, thanks to you, readers. I hope you had fun with this little read and enjoyed seeing some familiar faces. I can't wait for you to get to know the other guys of The Cardinals soon...

ABOUT THE AUTHOR

Claire Cain lives to eat and drink her way around the globe with her traveling soldier and three kids, but is perhaps even happier hunkered down at home in a pair of sweatpants and slippers using any free moment she has to read and cook. Or talk—she really likes to talk. She has become an expert at packing too many dishes in too few cabinets and making houses into homes from Utah to Germany and many places in between. She's a proud Army wife and is frankly just really happy to be here.

You can also join Claire's facebook reader group for exclusive content and fun: https://www.facebook.com/groups/clairecain/

Website: http://www.clairecainwriter.com

E-mail: Claire@ClaireCainWriter.com

Newsletter sign-up for new releases, exclusives, and freebies, including a free book:

http://www.clairecainwriter.com/newsletter

amazon.com/author/clairecain

bookbub.com/authors/claire-cain

instagram.com/clairecainwriter

facebook.com/clairecainwriter

goodreads.com/clairecainwriter

pinterest.com/clairecainwriter

tiktok.com/@clairecainwriter